THE DYING OF THE LIGHT

Robert Richardson was born in Manchester in 1940. Since 1960 he has been a journalist, working for many years on the *Daily Mail* and contributing to, among others, the *Independent*, the *Guardian* and the *Sunday Times*. He is married with two sons and lives in Old Hatfield. Robert Richardson is also the author of *The Latimer Mercy*, *Bellringer Street*, *The Book of the Dead* and *Sleeping in the Blood*; all of which are published by Gollancz.

THE DYING OF THE LIGHT

by

Robert Richardson

GOLLANCZ CRIME

For Lea and Pino

Gollancz Crime is an imprint of Victor Gollancz Ltd
14 Henrietta Street, London WC2E 8QJ

First published in Great Britain 1990
by Victor Gollancz Ltd

First Gollancz Crime edition 1991

A catalogue record for this book
is available from the British Library

ISBN 0-575-05091-8

Printed and bound in Great Britain
by Cox & Wyman Ltd, Reading

Do not go gentle into that good night,
Old age should burn and rave at close of day;
Rage, rage against the dying of the light.

Dylan Thomas
1914–1953

Author's note

Porthennis, the ancient name for the fishing village of Mousehole, has been resurrected — and given a different spelling — for this book and some liberties have been taken with Cornish geography. The disappearance of Ruth Adams in 1951, which has never been fully explained, is the only fragment of truth in a totally fictional story.

Chapter One

Blank eyes opaque as emerald marbles, Tess Davy lay on her back across the rock, body limp and still. A sand fly crawled over her cheek, a creeping black blemish on a frozen, fine-boned face of rose quartz pink. The sea breeze stirred long hair falling from her hanging head in a tawny cascade. The silence was filled by the seething hiss of waves endlessly rattling stones like an infinity of dice on the beach two hundred feet below the cliffs, mixed with choking sobs of gliding herring gulls swooping through sun-laden sapphire sky. As the shadow of one slid swiftly across her body and was gone, Augustus Maltravers's features were immobile and unreadable as he looked down at the terrified death mask of the woman he loved. A man stood over her. His name was Neil Levis and it was exactly six months since Tess had met him. He slowly raised his hands, staring at the powerful, trembling, sweat-glistening fingers with which he had mercilessly strangled her, as though unable to believe that it had happened. Then he shrieked like an animal in agony.

Two miles away, Martha Shaw lay on her studio floor, crushed from neck to waist by nearly two tons of granite, the statue she knew it had contained partly sculpted out of stubborn hardness in bright sparks and flying chips. Knuckles of one hand were tense and white on fingers squeezed in terror around a cold chisel. Her mouth stretched open wide, silent symbol of a scream stopped in her throat when the rock slammed down with a crash that had rattled the huge windows of the skylight so violently that several had shattered. The door of the studio was flung open and a woman burst in.

"Martha! Are you all right? I heard a bang and . . ." The sentence ended in a cry of horror at what she saw. "Martha!"

Crackled and loosened by the thunderous impact, another pane of the skylight gave way. Triangular shards of glass fell silently before shattering on the grey concrete floor in a cacophony of harsh bells, but the woman did not move.

"Martha?" Softly spoken now, calling the name was a pitiful plea for a miracle, a helpless disbelief that the irrefutable reality of savage death could somehow be undone. Grief flooded the woman's eyes, but she was too shocked for tears. As she remained as still as the corpse on the floor, a man ran in through the door which she had left open behind her.

"What's happened?" he demanded urgently. "I was at the top of the garden and saw you . . . Christ!"

For a long moment both of them stood together in silence, then he took the woman's arm and turned her away.

"Come on. There's nothing we can do. We'd better call the police."

Stunned and incapable of thought, the woman let him lead her out of the studio and across the garden to the adjacent cottage. The radio she had been listening to when the great slam of sound had reached her was still playing, Bach drifting through open windows and fading among bees and honeysuckle into warm, scented, birdsong air.

In his sitting-room, Mortimer Lacey shivered as some undefinable impression touched him, a draught chilled with ghostly ice coming from nowhere in the heat of the day. The tortoiseshell cat dozing on his lap growled and leapt down, abruptly agitated.

"It's all right, Tobias." He scooped the animal up, stroking it reassuringly. "It was only death again. You should be used to it by now."

He rose from his chair and crossed to the window, the cat still tense in his arms, and looked out towards the harbour. The seeping incoming tide was still low and holidaymakers' children shouted with delight as they ran among tilted boats marooned on sand smeared with a wide crescent of sea lettuce. A little girl knelt in a shallow half moon of water by the harbour entrance, solemnly filling a red plastic bucket and pouring its contents back, dreamy and fascinated by splash and ripple. A group of boys clung to the face of the harbour wall like monkeys, toes and fingers seeking cracks in joints between huge squared stones. Tourists — emmetts to the resident Cornish — strolled among crawling cars on the short, narrow Porthennis seafront, past souvenir shops, general store and the harbour office topped with a small clock tower. A yacht with sails bent like a tightened bow in an offshore breeze swept by against a distant horizon shimmering in heat haze. Late July, the benison of a sweltering day, slow, pacific and idle.

"Only death," Lacey repeated, long, thin fingers massaging the cat's head. "We've felt it before. But that was very close."

Calmed by attention and reassurance, Tobias relaxed, slipping back into tranquillity, at one again with the peace of high summer.

Siren whooping, the police car broke free of the labyrinth of packed streets and raced up Fern Hill, screeching to a halt opposite the gate of Martha Shaw's cottage. Two constables in shirt-sleeves leapt out and ran to the front door where the man was waiting to lead them to the studio. As they stood inside, the sound of an arriving ambulance reached them.

"Have you touched anything?" one of the policemen asked.

"No."

"Did you find her?"

"No. Ruth — Miss Harvey — did. She's in the cottage."

"Right." The officer turned to his colleague. "Call CID and explain to the ambulance crew, then guard the door. I'll go and talk to Miss Harvey."

Another woman was about to enter through the garden gate off the road as the second policeman returned to the patrol car.

"What's happened?" she demanded. "Is something wrong?"

"I'm afraid there's been an accident," the policeman told her. "I'm sorry, but I can't allow you to go in."

"What do you mean?" The woman sounded offended. "Miss Shaw and Miss Harvey are friends of mine. I may be able to help."

9

"There's nothing you can do. Please let us handle this." He turned to the ambulancemen, who were also standing by the gate. "There's a lady in the cottage. See what you can do for her. It's a CID job."

"CID?" the woman echoed. "What's going on? I insist you tell me!"

Short and stocky, she appeared to be well over seventy. Salt and pepper black and white hair was pulled into a bun at the back of her neck and the slackening skin of her face was browned with time and weather. A pair of spectacles hung from a gold chain against an embroidered peasant blouse. Despite her age, she was alert and pugnacious. The policeman classified her as a nosy old neighbour, determined not to be left out of some local drama, who would have to be firmly dealt with.

"Miss Shaw is dead," he told her bluntly. "Now please go back home and let us deal with it."

"Dead? That's ridiculous." The woman reacted as though he was lying just to get rid of her. "I was talking to her only this morning."

"Then you may be able to assist us in our inquiries," he said. "I have to radio headquarters and then I would like your name and address. Just wait one moment."

The prospect of becoming part of an official inquiry either excited the woman or made her think about the wisdom of too much insistence. She waited obediently as the policeman made his call on the car radio and appeared to have calmed down by the time he had finished.

"My name is Dorothy Lowe and I live in the next cottage down the hill." She indicated a house half hidden between trees in the adjoining garden. "I am an old friend of both Miss Shaw and Miss Harvey."

Sensing that her mood had changed, the officer wrote the information in his notebook and thanked her.

"I'll inform CID," he promised. "It may help them if you could be at home for the next hour or so."

"I'm not going anywhere." There was a flash of renewed tetchiness in the statement. "Miss Harvey will want to see me."

"We'll let her know of your concern."

They stood facing each other for a moment, then the woman turned and walked back down the hill. The policeman sighed philosophically. In a place like Porthennis, it would have been impossible to keep what had happened quiet for very long; the news would now be spread by Dorothy Lowe with additional speed.

Inside the cottage, Ruth Harvey sat on a straight chair in the back living-room, staring at the tiled fireplace. The horror of what had happened seemed to have shrivelled her, making her appear even smaller than she actually was. Brittle parchment skin, stretched across the little face that had carried the naïvety of infancy into old age, was stained with a waxy pallor, intensifying tiny crimson webs of veins on each cheek. Thin forearms, bare in her flowered cotton summer dress, were streaked with flour. An ambulanceman gently took one of her clasped hands from her lap and placed a cup of tea in it.

"Drink that," he said coaxingly. "It'll make you feel better."

The cup was accepted, but he had to make her raise it and sip the contents like a child. Since she had last spoken Martha Shaw's name she had not said a word and her silence remained absolute for twenty minutes before the CID arrived. Recognising her condition, Sergeant Richard Doughty finally coaxed out the name of her doctor and told one of the ambulancemen to call him. Then he went into the kitchen where the man who had escorted Ruth Harvey from the studio was waiting.

Like many dwarfs, Nick Charlton looked as though he had originally grown to full height before being compressed. Stumpy legs and muscular arms protruded clumsily from the barrel body and his face was like one drawn on a rubber ball then squeezed in a vice, features pinched and fighting for space. Short, tight curls of chocolate-coloured hair gave a further impression of restriction. He was wearing dirty bottle-green cord trousers, cut down from their original length, and an orange-check cotton shirt. Sitting at the plastic-topped table, only the upper half of his chest was visible. Doughty took the other chair, noting details of his name and address before asking what to his knowledge had happened.

"I was in the vegetable garden. Up there." Charlton gestured through the window. The garden climbed steeply from the back of the cottage and Doughty could see rows of bean sticks at the far end. "I thought I heard a crash, then I saw Miss Harvey running to the studio. I came down and saw what had happened. I brought her back here and called the police."

Bald and informative, the statement was unemotional. The accent was not Cornish and Doughty mentally noted distinct London sounds.

"Are you the regular gardener?" he asked.

"I am now. Someone else used to do it, but he died. I started coming here regular this year."

"It's a big garden," Doughty observed. "They must have needed help."

"They're both getting on as well," Charlton added. "And Miss Shaw was always busy in her studio."

Doughty's local knowledge told him all he needed to know about Martha Shaw's life, so he concentrated on her death.

"Could you see the studio from where you were working?"

"Yes, but I wasn't looking. I was knelt down picking lettuces and facing the other way anyway."

"So you didn't see if anyone went in before you heard the crash?" Doughty added another question without waiting for a reply. "Where did Miss Harvey run from?"

"The cottage. Where else?"

Doughty did not reply as he scribbled the answer down and stood up.

"Thank you, Mr Charlton. We'll require an official statement from you. One of my colleagues will take it." He walked towards the door.

"Is Miss Harvey all right?" Charlton's enquiry sounded awkward.

"She's very shocked of course, but her doctor has been called," Doughty replied. In the hall he told a detective constable to take Charlton's statement and stepped out of the front door as another car drew up and the police doctor climbed out. Doughty led him to the studio where he began to examine the body as best he could. As he waited, Doughty looked round the room; he would not touch anything until the Scene of Crime officer had arrived and completed his work. Martha Shaw's studio was made of wooden planking, a plain, high box with the skylight occupying most of the ceiling. In one corner stood some large packing cases and the furnishings consisted of a decrepit easy chair, tilted at an angle by the loss of one clawfoot wooden leg. Assorted hammers, chisels and other sculpting tools were scattered across a trestle table. There was only the one door. The floor was covered with splinters of stone and rock dust, smothered in random shoeprints clearly visible to the naked eye let alone forensic examination. Doughty forced himself to look at the body again. The eyes were stretched wide, as open and terrified as the mouth, and the right leg was trapped under the bottom rung of an old tubular metal stepladder fallen beside the corpse.

"Dead," the doctor announced with protective mortuary humour. "Very. But not for very long."

"We know that." Doughty glanced at his watch. "We got the call just after it happened less than three quarters of an hour ago."

The doctor straightened up. "Well I can't examine her properly until you get her out from under this lot. How long will you be?"

"A couple of hours or so at least," Doughty replied.

"Let me know when you're ready." He snapped his bag shut and nodded at the body. "Martha Shaw, eh? What a bloody ironic way for her to go. She's going to make a few headlines."

He stepped across the floor and looked at the ladder. "That's a death trap in itself. She must have been mad standing on it."

"They say they're all mad," Doughty commented.

"But it takes a lot to kill 'em." Absently whistling the judge's song from *Trial by Jury* — he was a leading light in Penzance amateur operatics — the doctor walked out into the sunshine.

"You know," Maltravers remarked reflectively, "if she'd only told him in act three that the handkerchief was at the laundry, she'd have avoided an awful lot of domestic unpleasantness."

Helen Finch appeared surprised. "I never thought I'd hear you knock Shakespeare. You quote him often enough."

"Just a minor criticism of construction. He'll survive."
Maltravers nodded at the seamless sky above the Botallack
Theatre. "He survived that air assault."

"One of the hazards of playing this place," Helen agreed.

They were sitting on the lowest of the precipitous grass-
covered terraces at the foot of a natural semi-circular amphitheatre that made up the auditorium of the Botallack on top of
the cliffs. In front of them, an empty open-air stage stood against
a curved, flat backdrop of glittering blue and silver sea, sweeping
round three quarters of the horizon. Draped curtains and
furniture transformed pillars and arches of grey Cornish rock
into an imitation of Italy. It was a stunning setting for high
drama, although Othello's eloquent defence of Desdemona's
wooing before the Duke of Venice and his court had been
shatteringly interrupted when an Isles of Scilly helicopter had
clattered overhead. More than fifty years earlier, when Agnes
Thorpe had defied ridicule by building a theatre on the very
edge of the ragged clifftops above a chaotic shoreline of tumbled
boulders, such difficulties had not been anticipated. Not that
they would have deflected Agnes; a dream born when she had
first stood at the spot had grown into an obsession and a
personal pilgrimage. Now her statue witnessed its subsequent
success and what she would have regarded as the natural
consequence of a purblind world's inevitable acceptance of a
vision. Every summer the Botallack played to audiences who
suffered personal discomfort and vagaries of weather for the
experience of witnessing drama performed in conditions as near
to its Greek roots as could be conceived.

Leading stars were rare at the Botallack, but talented actors
and actresses were often attracted to productions which mixed
classics and less demanding but quality works. As well as
Shakespeare, the current season included *Private Lives*, *Lady
Windermere's Fan*, *Hobson's Choice* and *A Little Night Music*.
Having seen a new play which she had expected to keep her
employed for several months collapse under critical overkill
(wearing his playwright's hat, Maltravers had warned her it
would), Tess Davy had jumped at the alternative to enforced
resting of playing Desdemona one week, followed by Coward's

Amanda Prynne—an interesting contrast in marital difficulties. Neil Levis, an actor who had become a friend, was sharing the experience, appearing first as jealous Moor and then worldly Elyot Chase.

As they waited for Tess to join them, Maltravers leaned against the terrace, turning over agreeable memories as he looked at the back of Helen's head, boiling bubbles of chestnut hair flecked with blonde highlights which he suspected camouflaged creeping drifts of grey. They were cousins, but only in a long-distant sort of way; the relationship had been far enough apart for them to have had a no-commitment affair several years earlier, before they each entered disastrous marriages with other people. Helen was thirty-four, her slightly Oriental face with its scatter of honey freckles Westernised by wide, toffee-brown eyes. After her divorce, her share of the profits from selling a Docklands flat had enabled her to buy a cottage in Porthennis, working as a secretary to supplement an erratic income as a painter. Maltravers and she had not seen each other for more than a year, although they kept vaguely in touch by letter.

"What happened to . . . What was his name? . . . Gerald something or other?" he asked idly. "I had the impression that was getting serious."

"Didn't I tell you?" Helen did not look round. "It ran into some problems. Specifically a wife and two children in Plymouth that he somehow forgot to mention."

"Oh, dear. How did you find out?"

"I had a phone call." Helen turned to him, cynical amusement on her face as she pushed bright, pink-framed glasses back into position on the bridge of her nose. "From another lady who thought I ought to know he was screwing her as well. We had quite an interesting chat."

"Not another one," Maltravers protested. "You've developed a virtual genius for choosing ratfink boyfriends. He must be about the tenth."

"I chose you once." Helen looked nostalgically at very blue eyes and unexpectedly feminine mouth contrasting with slightly flawed, quasi-Grecian features. "I should have hung on in there."

"That was long ago and in another country," Maltravers reminded her.

"But the wench is not dead." Tess was regarding them amusedly from the stage. "There's been enough passion around here this afternoon without you two fanning old flames."

"Don't play quotations with me," Maltravers warned her. "You know I'm better at it than you are. I have been faithful to thee, Cynara . . . And you can complete that one as well if you want."

"Well you can bet your sweet life that my shadow's going to fall between your lips and hers like the wrath of God, whoever she is," Tess countered drily.

She flopped down next to him and lay back, closing her eyes as she raised Raphaelesque face to shining sky. Slender, tanned, naked legs stretched from cream shorts in a manner which would have ruined the already troubled reputation of Brabantio's daughter.

"Why do people bring young children on a day like this? If I'd been dragged off at that age to watch Shakespeare when I could have been on the beach, I'd have thrown up."

"One of them did," Maltravers told her. "Trying to keep it quiet with chocolate and ice cream wasn't a good idea. Didn't you notice?"

"There's so much happening in the audience in the afternoons you have to work hard to ignore it," Tess replied. "Most of the time it's the seagulls that worry us. They tell endless stories about surprisingly accurate droppings."

"It's said to be good luck," said Maltravers.

"Not in the middle of a speech it isn't. At least we didn't have to worry about the weather today. Michael Church told me he once played the first act of *The Master Builder* in a downpour."

Maltravers nodded sympathetically. "Anyone who could build a theatre like this in a climate like ours has to be mad. English eccentricity at its finest."

"It's still an incredible place to play," Tess said. "When it's right here, it's unbelievable. Tonight it will be an audience of grown ups and a beautiful evening. Why don't you come again?"

"It's booked solid," Maltravers reminded her. "Even sleeping with the leading lady can't find me a seat. Anyway, your corpse is too lifelike for my peace of mind. I'll pick you up at the end. Come on, you've got three hours to recover."

They climbed deep steps, through a gate and past the box office to the car-park. Maltravers drove out to where the road immediately dropped, twisting along the cliffs overlooking Porthennis. Miniaturised by distance, its houses fell among trees in a crumpled fan shape from sliding moors and farmland to the focal point of the harbour, stone walls curved like open pincers. From the highest point they could see clear across Mounts Bay, the great scoop of sea grasped in a huge claw where England pushed to its extreme points west and south. Distant white seafront hotels catching the sun, Penzance shone in the claw's palm, then vanished as they dropped towards the old fishing village, its population swollen for a few summer months by tourists. The approaches to Porthennis dwindled from narrow roads to single car lanes until a coiled and knotted network of alleyways and streets shadowy between granite houses barely ten feet apart in places meant that second gear constituted reckless driving. Crawling down Fern Hill into the outskirts, Maltravers stopped to let a delivery van through where a police car and another vehicle blocked half the road.

"That's Martha and Ruth's cottage." Helen peered at two men standing by the front door. Another man emerged from a high white clapboard building further along the lane and crossed the garden to speak to them.

"Who are Martha and Ruth?" Maltravers asked.

"Martha's a sculptor and Ruth's her friend," Helen replied. "Her very good friend. They've lived here for years. But what's happened?"

"Do you want to go and ask?"

"I'll call Dorothy when we get back. She'll know."

"And if she doesn't, somebody will tell you in the Steamer tonight," Maltravers added as he drove on. "Nothing happens in Porthennis that the public bar isn't aware of."

He cautiously negotiated the maze past the harbour that took them back to Lifeboat Row, half a dozen cottages set at right angles to the beach, originally built for the lifeboat captain and crew. Their walls had been patiently fitted together from different sizes of stone, making them all subtly different, unlike newer homes built out of regular, machine-cut blocks. Helen opened the stable-style front door and picked up the telephone as Tess went upstairs for a shower and Maltravers headed for the kitchen to make tea.

Number One Lifeboat Row had originally been the home of the skipper, presumably a man with a diminutive wife and one child; a family of more than three in such a tiny two-up, two-down would have been uncomfortably crowded. The ground floor rooms had now been knocked into one, a plain wooden plank — dignified with the status of a beam in estate agent's hyperbole — running across the ceiling to reveal where the divide had been. It was furnished with Helen's share of the salvage of her marriage. A 1930s Tudor-copy court cupboard; circular rosewood dining table with Baroque-style centre pedestal and tapestry seat chairs; hooded leather club porter's seat and carved mahogany lyre-back chair facing each other by the wood-burning stove; Edwardian chaise-longue with wine-dark velvet and original brass studs and two bulbous easy chairs. Rough plaster walls were crowded with Helen's own water-colours and pen and ink sketches of cats, mixed with tinted West Country prints and assorted other pictures and the stone floor was covered with fitted plain avocado green broadloom carpet. It was an ad hoc collection no interior designer would have put together, but it worked.

In the kitchen, little bigger than a telephone kiosk tacked on the back, Maltravers heard Helen twice ring off and redial as he measured Lapsang tea into a plump brown pot — Helen loathed tea-bags — and waited for the kettle. Then she spoke for a few moments and he was pouring in the water when she appeared in the doorway.

"I've tried Dorothy and Belvedere, but there's no reply," she explained. "Edward's at his shop, but says he's heard nothing."

Maltravers shrugged. "Accident perhaps?"

"I didn't see an ambulance."

"We don't know when whatever it was happened. It could have gone. Tell me more about . . . Martha and Ruth was it?"

Helen took a tin from the fridge to satisfy a ragamuffin cat giving the unlikely impression it had not been fed for a week.

"Martha was one of the founders of what was called the Porthennis School," she said. "Just after the war a whole group of artists settled here. They were quite fashionable at one time. The best known was the painter Frank Morgan, who exhibited at the Royal Academy, and Martha has built up a reputation as a sculptor in recent years. Here, piglet."

She stroked the cat as it began to eat. "She's had commissions from firms in London who want something for their receptions. You know the sort of thing. Commercialism making a token gesture towards art. Several of her pieces have been sold to America as well."

Maltravers began pouring the tea. "And Ruth?"

"Very bad poet, very nice lady. Doesn't earn a penny of course, but she's been Martha's lover for ever — they're both in their seventies now — and Martha makes enough to keep them both."

"And how did Porthennis react to the arrival of a couple of lesbians?" Maltravers asked. "People were still getting hot under the collar about *The Well of Loneliness* in the 1940s."

"I don't imagine it occurred to anyone at the time. All the Porthennis School were considered fairly mad. The men had long hair and the women read the Webbs and Russell and believed in free love with birth control. It was sort of a Bloomsbury-on-Sea. They were ahead of their time round here. By the time the locals worked out the relationship between Martha and Ruth, society had caught up and it didn't matter."

They went back into the sitting-room. Sunlight streamed through the top half of the front door Helen had left open and sounds of activity from the harbour faintly reached them.

"Does the School still flourish?" Maltravers asked.

"They kid themselves it does," Helen said. "It was the big thing in their lives, but Martha is the only one who's made it apart from Frank Morgan, and that was years ago."

"Is it why you chose Porthennis? Because of the artists?"

"Partly, but the real reason is that I used to love coming here on holiday. I remember some of them from when I was little.

Belvedere Scott used to do his Augustus John act in those days, painting on the harbour front in a felt hat and filthy smock. He claimed to lay at least ten women during the season . . . He made a pass at Mummy once when we stopped to watch him." Helen laughed in recollection. "He growled something about wanting to paint her naked straight after he'd ravished her."

Maltravers had an instant image of Helen's mother, pillar of the Women's Institute, matronly rectitude in sensible shoes, put on earth for the sole purpose of being the suburban bank manager's wife she inevitably became. "What did she tell him?"

Helen paused, then quoted. "'I beg your pardon, sir, but I am a respectable married woman and this is my daughter!' I must have been about twelve at the time. Belvedere leered at me and said something I didn't understand about unripe fruit. After that we started going to Eastbourne."

Maltravers grinned. "Does he still carry on like that?"

"Only out of habit. He's turned eighty now. Most of the time he just cons drinks out of visitors with stories about what he and Picasso used to get up to in Paris. All lies of course, but nobody minds."

Maltravers heard the latch click on the front gate and someone walking up the short path to the door, but from where he was sitting he could not see who it was.

"Helen? Are you home?" The voice was male, but light and gently modulated. She twisted round in her chair.

"Hello, Mortimer. You're back. Come in." There was the sound of the bottom half of the door being opened.

Maltravers never forgot his first impression of Mortimer Lacey, the figure carried with natural elegance, erect head crowned by perfectly coiffured grey hair. He could have been aged anything between fifty and seventy — as it turned out, he was fifty-eight — and the gaunt face, swarthy skin tight over hollows exaggerating pointed nose, was straight out of a Phiz drawing. He was wearing pencil-grey slacks and pale-blue shirt with a matching paisley pattern cravat. His neck was chicken-thin, and bony wrists tapered into slender fingers with mani-cured nails. Matching Maltravers's six feet, he would have been emaciated by the loss of a single ounce of flesh. Deep-violet eyes turned to Maltravers, who had the unnerving feeling that he was being instantly analysed. For a moment the eyes pierced, then filled with warmth.

"Hello. You are a friend of Helen's."

Maltravers was conscious of the phrasing as he took the extended skeletal hand. Not "you must be", but "you are"; a statement of fact instead of the usual supposition. The eyes twinkled and Maltravers's sense of caution heightened; it was as though his interpretation had been picked up and he was being silently complimented on his awareness. Lacey released his hand and sat on the chaise-longue.

"I got home last night," he told Helen. "Your lights were still on, but it was late so I didn't call."

"You should have. I wanted you to meet Gus and Tess." Helen turned to Maltravers. "This is Mortimer Lacey, my next-door neighbour. This is Gus Maltravers and . . . and this is Tess Davy his girlfriend." Tess appeared at the bottom of the stairs running behind the wall in one corner of the room. "She's playing Desdemona at the Botallack this week."

"Of course." Lacey stood up, took Tess's hand and kissed it. The gesture indefinably escaped affectation. "I am going tonight and am greatly looking forward to it."

"Thank you." Tess regarded him guardedly and Maltravers knew she had also immediately sensed something about Lacey's personality which intrigued her. "I hope you enjoy it."

"I'm sure I will, just as I would enjoy a cup of tea." Lacey smiled impishly at Helen.

"Coming up." Helen walked towards the kitchen. "How was London?"

"Nasty, brutish and much, much too long," Lacey replied as he sat down again. "I can't imagine now how I once enjoyed it so much. It's not the same place of course. Places never are."

"Oh." Helen stopped by the kitchen door and looked back at him. "Have you heard anything about what's happened at Martha and Ruth's? We saw a police car outside the cottage when we came back this afternoon."

Maltravers instinctively turned to Lacey as Helen asked the question and saw the spasm of something slip in and out of his eyes. Shock? Fear? Grief? It was replaced by a cold, almost grim, acceptance.

"Martha?" he repeated softly. "I knew it was close."

"Pardon?" Helen said. "Knew what was close?"

Lacey waved the question aside. "It doesn't matter. Do you know any more?"

"No. I've tried ringing a few people, but nobody seems to know anything. There must have been an accident."

"Perhaps, but . . ." Lacey appeared to be talking to himself, almost as though the rest of them were no longer there. "Could it have been?"

After a moment he shook his head then stood up abruptly and went to stare out of the window, hands clasped behind his back. Maltravers frowned at Tess and Helen, but they all remained silent until Lacey spoke again without turning round.

"Whatever's happened, I'm sorry to have to tell you that Martha Shaw is dead."

Silence returned, then Maltravers broke it. "You seem very certain."

"I am. I felt her die."

Chapter Two

Spontaneous song burst through the public bar of the Steamer, baritones and basses combining in a chorus of West Country defiance in support of a Bishop of Bristol imprisoned by James II for opposing legislation granting greater religious tolerance for those who did not share his Grace's image of God; the Porthennis Male Voice Choir — including several Nonconformists whom the Bishop would presumably have hanged given the opportunity — were relaxing after their Friday night rehearsal.

> And do they know the where and when?
> And shall Trelawny die?
> There's twenty thousand Cornishmen
> Will know the reason why.

The singing did not interrupt relentless chatter and clamour between stone walls and dark panelled wooden partitions beneath a low anaglypta ceiling pickled nicotine yellow by years of pipe and cigarette smoke. Beer gushed from taps beneath decorated porcelain hand pumps, glasses clinked, dominoes clattered as they were shuffled on a table in one corner. Coarse laughter at a joke involving the unlikely sexual encounter of a monk and a female trapeze artist mingled with a barmaid yelling the number of someone's food order and the rattle of falling coins marked the computer-regulated appearance of three pears in the windows of the fruit machine. Behind customers crammed round the bar, people shouted drinks orders above the racket. Visitors and locals jostled together, a liberal attitude towards children on licensed premises adding the raucous crying of a baby and an adolescent argument over some board game brought along to amuse teenagers while the adults enjoyed themselves. Squeezing between bodies with his pint and Helen's vodka and lime, Maltravers indicated the door leading outside with a movement of his head and took their drinks across the narrow street to where an iron rail topped the harbour wall.

The tide was in and gulls rode between rocking cabin cruisers, rowing boats and a two-masted yacht, dripping mooring ropes creaking as they tightened and fell slack again. A boy and girl paddled a blue and yellow inflatable dinghy, peering into the water for crabs. The sky was a translucent shell of ivory, mint green and pale turquoise as the sun gathered and flushed as it lay down behind the headland to their right. Holidaymakers on evening walks strolled past, tired after a day spent on beaches, walking moors or visiting theme parks. The muffled cacophony from inside the Steamer amplified the air of quietness.

"Curiouser and curiouser." Maltravers swallowed a mouthful of beer as he gazed across to the entrance gap in the harbour wall. "Martha Shaw was killed when a half-finished statue fell on top of her and Mortimer instantly knew it had happened half a mile away."

"All he knew was that someone had died suddenly," Helen corrected. "He only knew it was Martha when I told him what we'd seen."

"But all we saw was a police car outside her cottage," he argued. "There could have been other explanations. It's only in the last hour that you've managed to confirm it. But Mortimer wanders in and calmly announces that Martha is actually dead. And I'm quite prepared to believe he never left his cottage or made any phone calls."

Helen flicked a fragment of rust from seawater corrosion coating the railing. "Mortimer's fey. He can do things nobody can explain. His grandmother was a gipsy, and not one of your diddicoys and tinkers. Guaranteed Romany."

"Very old magic," Maltravers commented.

"Do you believe in it?"

"I don't disbelieve in it. Superstitions used to be gospel." He turned round and leaned back against the railing, looking up at the high walls of the Steamer. A slate plaque on the wall near the

24

door commemorated seven lifeboatmen who had died violently and valiantly when their vessel had been smashed to splinters in a merciless storm. "Is he a pure gipsy as well or did the family intermarry with the gorgios?"

"The what?"

"Gorgios. What gipsies call people like us. You, incidentally, are a mort or a rakli, which is a woman, and you used to be a monishai — Romany for wife."

Helen looked impressed. "Any more?"

"Muskra is the police and kushti bok means good luck."

"Where on earth did you learn all that?"

"I had to buy a lot of pegs. Anyway, tell me more about Mortimer."

"By the time he was born, his family had settled somewhere in London — Romford I think — so they must have sold the caravans. Mortimer was the gifted one, went to art school and became a successful clothes designer in the sixties. He was quite at home with the Flower Children."

"How long's he been here?"

"He bought the cottage years ago, but only moved when he got bored with it all. He never married, but I don't think he's gay, just not very interested in sex. By the time I arrived he had blended in with the scenery, another of the Porthennis eccentrics."

They pressed themselves against the railing as a minibus edged its way past, inches from their feet.

"I look forward to talking to him again," said Maltravers. "Very interesting character, even if he is uncomfortable company."

"Oh, yes," Helen said feelingly. "He's been very good to me, but it was a long time before I could relax with him and . . . Hello, Belvedere!"

A bulky, shabby brown tent with legs paused on the step from the street into the Steamer before slowly revolving. The front view resembled Ernest Hemingway about ten years after he died, lost vigour in advanced decay. Coarse stubble formed the unbuilt-on foundations of a beard and straggly hair fell from the back of an egg-brown bald head. Watery, blue eyes in a face creased and flaky as antique leather peered suspiciously before the features contorted into what was presumably friendly recognition, but would have frightened the nervous. Hand like an immense knot in thick rope grasped an ash walking stick as the figure rolled across the narrow space between them.

"Helen." The greeting given in a voice perfect for making indecent telephone calls, Scott's attention transferred to Maltravers. "Who's this then? New lover boy? Keeps you satisfied does he?"

"Drop the old lecher act, Belvedere," Helen told him sharply. "Gus isn't an emmett. He's a very good friend of mine."

"What do you think of the gnat's piss?" Scott nodded at Maltravers's pint disparagingly. "Wouldn't get a nun drunk."

"So what will you have?" Maltravers asked mildly. "Meths on the rocks? Or do you take it with a dash of Worcester sauce?"

Teeth strikingly resembling a half empty box of dates appeared repulsively as Scott laughed approvingly. "Like your friend, Helen. Rum. And say it's for me. They won't charge you any more, but you'll get more than a bloody dribble."

"I'll have him sorted out by the time you get back," Helen promised and Maltravers heard her talking sternly to the posturing artist as he went back into the Steamer. The crowd inside had become even noisier with the choir now singing requests, mainly for songs associated with drunken rugby players. Above roars of delight at increasingly suggestive lyrics, he managed to place his order and was impressed by the amount of rum he received for the price of a single.

"Tell the old bugger he still owes me twenty quid," the landlord shouted above the din as he handed Maltravers the glass. "If you can get it out of him, you can have a half."

"No promises." Holding the glass above the sardine-packed crowd, Maltravers fought his way out again. Helen and Scott had moved further round the harbour and were sitting on a bench, the old man with his stick clenched in both hands upright in front of him.

"That looks like it." One hand uncoiled and took the rum. "Helen says I've got to apologise. Don't know why, but I'm sorry for whatever it was." The glass was waved in a gesture which could have passed as an apology and half its contents vanished.

"I've been asking Belvedere about Martha," Helen said as Maltravers sat down. "He's got more details. Start again."

"Ruth heard a bloody great crash from the studio in the middle of the afternoon," he explained. "Dashed in and found her flattened under that statue she was working on. Bloody great lump of the Grampians. Can't have felt a thing. The police took Ruth to Penzance to give a statement. She's in a right two and eight. Dottie's looking after her."

"We saw the police there on our way back from the theatre," Helen said. "I tried ringing Dorothy, but there was no reply."

"Probably unplugged the telephone," Scott said dismissively. "She's always doing that."

"And the rest of you all seemed to be out," Helen added.

"Not me," Scott corrected. "I was sleeping off lunchtime."

Maltravers detected a note of satisfaction. Belvedere Scott clearly took a pride in his continuing capacity for alcohol.

"You've given us the edited highlights," he observed. "But does anyone know how it happened? Lumps of granite don't usually fall over unless there's a particularly strong wind."

"Must have done," Scott grunted. "Just fallen over. She wouldn't have pulled it on top of herself even if she could. The floor probably gave way under the weight. Riddled with rot that studio. Stupid cow."

Maltravers frowned. "You don't seem very upset. Helen's told me you and Martha had known each other for years."

"I've known everybody for years." Scott sourly took another swig of rum. "The older you get, the more deaths there are and the less you worry. We're all a day nearer the tomb than we were last night."

Having dismissed his lack of sorrow with fatalistic philosophy, he looked mournful for a moment. "Damned waste, though. She was a good artist, Mattie. Lot of work left in her."

"I must write to Ruth," Helen said. "Martha was what kept her going. She even used to encourage her over her poetry. That's love for you."

Apparently uncomfortable at an expression of genuine emotion, Scott finished his rum, leaned heavily on his stick and heaved himself up. "I'm going inside for a refill."

Maltravers watched him clumping back towards the Steamer. "You know, I bet if you scratch that crusty, boorish surface, underneath there beats a heart of pure stone."

"You've got him in one," Helen confirmed. "The old guard keep their secrets, but I've picked up enough to learn that. Belvedere's tolerated because he's old, but he can still be unforgivable at times."

"J B Priestley said the British will respect anything if it's been around long enough," Maltravers remarked. "And he looks as though he's one half of a pair who came down the gangplank of the Ark."

"Please, not a pair. One Belvedere's quite enough, thank you." Helen finished her drink. "But perhaps he has some excuses."

"Spare me artistic temperament," Maltravers warned. "The rule is, the less the talent, the greater the conceit."

"But Belvedere is — or was — talented," Helen replied. "He had an exhibition in London in the twenties which was a sensation. One critic described him as the greatest new painter in Europe."

"What happened?"

Helen shrugged. "Nobody knows now. He just . . . vanished. Perhaps he had a breakdown or something. Whatever it was, nobody heard anything about him for years, then he resurfaced in Porthennis. Dorothy arrived with him. They were lovers, but then they fell out and started living apart."

"Does he still paint?" Maltravers asked.

"Yes, but only the sort of pictures you find on chocolate boxes."

Maltravers sniffed. "All right, so he may have reasons to be bitter. But I still expected more sorrow over Martha's death, not just for an artist, but for an old friend."

"But you only have friends if you can love people. Belvedere doesn't love anyone. Not even himself."

★

The rest of the audience had gone as Mortimer Lacey waited by his car, darkness deepening over the Botallack. Beyond a fence opposite him, Agnes Thorpe's statue held a glow of old rose as a blood-orange sun slid behind the sea. Crickets were loud in the silence and miles above an airliner drew a line of pink chalk across dusky, mauve sky. He heard voices up the slope from the theatre then Tess appeared, calling goodnight to other members of the cast, before joining him.

"This is very kind of you," she said. "Gus would have come."

"Quite unnecessary when I was here already." He took her hand. "It was a wonderful performance. There's magic in the Botallack, but not everyone finds it. You did."

"I could hardly fail tonight. Before I went on, someone said the audience was dead right and they were with me all the way."

"Perhaps one more than the rest." Lacey released her hand. "Desdemona is trapped by evil which eventually destroys her. That happened in real life today."

Tess's eyes narrowed as she tried to make out the expression on his face, half in shadow against the purpling night.

"What are you talking about?"

"Martha Shaw." He paused. "You must forgive me, but it's been a rather emotional day and Shakespeare at full throttle has . . . amplified certain matters. Do you mind if we look at the view for a moment?"

They walked across the car-park and over the grass of the clifftops until only the sea lay stretched before them. Breeze carrying a tang of brine rustled through the grass. There was a distant sound of waves flicking against rocks and far off to the east the Lizard lighthouse blinked a pinprick of yellow in grey gloom. Tess waited as Lacey gazed at the vanishing line where sky and water met.

"Martha Shaw was murdered," he said finally without looking at her. It was a quiet statement of fact.

"How do you know that?" Tess demanded. "You can't be so certain."

"Yes I can."

"Then who did it?"

"That I don't know."

29

"Then you're guessing." She looked at him uncertainly. "Aren't you?"

"No." Lacey's shoulders rose and fell as he sighed very deeply. "But I'm afraid I'll have to prove that I'm not."

He hesitated, as though unhappy about something. Tess felt suddenly apprehensive as he turned to her again, shadowed face sombre.

"I don't know how long ago it happened, but you and Gus were once involved with a young woman who had been wickedly hurt by her husband. You helped to save her from him and promised you would never tell anyone what had happened." Finely-drawn eyebrows mutely sought confirmation. "I'm right, aren't I?"

"Go on." Tess's reply was guarded. "What else do you know?"

"It concerned a human skeleton. Is that enough?"

Not enough; it was too much. For a moment Tess stood very still then shivered with the shock of it. Apart from herself and Maltravers, the grotesque details of the Bellringer Street nightmare were known by only two people. It was virtually impossible Lacey could have met either of them and, even if he had, it was unthinkable they would have told him.

"You can't . . ." Her voice gulped in her tightened throat. "You can't know that. You *mustn't* know that!"

"At one point this evening, you used the memory of it to amplify your emotions," Lacey continued. "It's a common trick of your profession. It was very brief but very intense, because you needed something powerful to help you deliver a line. I caught it."

"Caught it?" Tess demanded. "What do you mean?"

"I saw it with you. Not the whole story, because you only conjured up its most potent effects. I know nothing more than what I've told you. No names or places or details. But I know it happened. Now do you believe me when I say Martha Shaw was murdered?"

Tess instinctively stepped away from him. Her voice had dropped to a whisper. "How dangerous are you, Mortimer?"

"I'm not dangerous at all. I have no power over people, I can't read thoughts at random. I have not sold my soul to the devil." Teeth gleamed as he smiled in the darkness. "I am Mortimer

Lacey, retired fashion designer of Number Two Lifeboat Row, Porthennis, Cornwall. Generally regarded as a harmless eccentric and slanderously suspected of being queer. I have never to my knowledge harmed anyone in my life."

"But you're bloody good at frightening."

"Then I'm very sorry, but I have no choice. When I met you and Gus this afternoon — after Martha had died — I knew that both of you and Helen would become involved in her death . . . Don't ask how, just believe me. All I can do is help as best I can, and to do that I had to convince you of certain things about me."

High beam headlights leapt out of the dark as a car appeared on the lane past the theatre, illuminating them both for an instant, before disappearing again as the vehicle dropped into another dip. Tess felt reassured that the twentieth century was still within running distance.

"I'd like you to take me back," she said. "I need to talk to Gus."

"Of course you do."

In the car, Lacey did not speak as Tess watched night-washed hedges and stone walls flow by. As they reached the first streetlamps on the edge of Porthennis, she began to feel better. A conversation such as she had just had lost some of its potency under sodium lights.

"Will you come in and tell Gus what you've told me?" she asked as they reached Helen's cottage.

"No, but I'll see him tomorrow. You must both talk about it first." Lacey bowed slightly. "Your performance tonight was superb. I have seen . . . it must be eight Desdemonas, but have never been as moved before. Thank you. It was a privilege to be there. Goodnight."

Tess remained at Helen's gate as Lacey walked the few paces to his own cottage and let himself in. He did not look back. As he closed the door, she gazed over roofs that fell from Lifeboat Row to where water in the silent harbour glittered under necklaces of silver bulbs hung in loops between posts. On Danes Isle, a low, craggy outcrop of rock just offshore, barely visible in the darkness, a seagull squawked as it settled for the night. From the Crab and Anchor, Porthennis's other pub which stood on higher ground behind Lifeboat Row, a woman shouted something Tess could not make out. Tomorrow would be another day of the holidays, a matinée with children fidgeting, resenting loss of time spent on sea and sand, then the final Saturday evening performance. Television, radio and newspapers would report the latest twists of a salacious political scandal, developments in a national industrial dispute and a continuing outbreak of listeria. People would come to Porthennis to take snapshots, buy postcards and gifts and enjoy cream teas. Tess would wake up knowing that the man on the other side of her bedroom wall, using powers she could not comprehend, was convinced — no, *knew* — a woman had been murdered. And the most terrifying thing about it was that she believed him.

Belvedere Scott was drunk. He weaved through the murky alleyway, cursing as he stumbled; dim and misleading, light seeped through drawn curtains of houses close on either side. His stick's metal ferrule struck sparks off cobbles as his ungainly body slithered down a wall and he sat in uncomprehending bewilderment, wheezing noisily before he momentarily fell asleep. Some instant dream invaded his mind and he woke with a half shout that echoed and faded; nobody in the houses either heard or bothered to investigate. Great bearpaw of a hand straining on the wrought-iron handrail of front steps which bent under his weight, he struggled to his feet and lumbered on. His cottage was half-way up the hillside overlooking Porthennis, at the top of a steep flight of rough steps overhung with thick summer bushes, leaves and creepers brushing his face and clothes as he staggered clumsily upwards. He stopped as a figure appeared ten feet ahead of him, dark as the shadows out of which it stepped. Scott swayed, squinting through gloom and branches, alcohol-muddled mind unable to interpret, mouth working dumbly as he struggled to form words.

"Mattie?" he finally mumbled. "Sod off. You're dead. I'm pissed."

He waved an arm dismissively across his body, warding off a

spectral presence as he started to climb again. The figure remained. Convinced in his intoxication that it would either vanish or he would walk straight through it, Scott continued upwards. It was another bad Friday night.

Then the figure leapt forward and pushed him violently.

Scott's arms flailed empty air as he teetered crazily like a clown on a tightrope before toppling backwards, a wild flapping black ball wrapped in his flowing cloak. Hands snatched desperately at branches, but his weight snapped and tore them, leaves and twigs scattering in the wake of his tumbling momentum. The back of his head struck the sharp edge of a stone step as he clumsily somersaulted and his stick, caught in the folds of his cloak, ripped the material. Towards the bottom, the pathway widened and his body turned sideways, rolling over and over, before coming to a stop. He groaned, then lay still, face down in a pool of pale lemon light cast by a lamppost. Up the rise of the steps, the figure had vanished.

Chapter Three

Hopping on and off strategically placed stools, Nick Charlton scuttled about his kitchen preparing breakfast. His house, in a terrace squeezed into the intersecting tangle of tiny streets behind the harbour front, could have been built for his dimensions; low ceilings, cramped rooms, stairs designed in miniature, no sense of space. Inside, cheap functional furniture stood on worn carpets or bare linoleum; outside needed painting. The unexpected contrast was the front garden, abundant with French marigold, blood-crimson fuchsia, golden nasturtium, dusk-pink geranium, flourishing and cared for in a nest of low brick walls.

Sitting on a tall bar-stool, Charlton read the morning paper propped up against the radio blaring pop music on the table as he ate. It was not the sort of paper which would report Martha Shaw's death; its readers had never heard of her. He paused at the statutory picture on page three, carnal female perfection artificially created by patient hours in a photographic studio; provocative smile, promising eyes, casually displayed breasts, flawless naked skin. Such women were not available to men cruelly stunted by nature, another tormenting reminder to underline his physical restrictions.

Years earlier he had worked as a circus clown, perpetual greasepaint smile masking hatred of laughing audiences; a cripple forced to dance as a grotesque, a lunatic taunted behind bars at Bedlam. When his mother died, guilt-wracked with a false conviction of responsibility for his condition, she had left him a small unmortgaged house and a surprisingly large insurance policy, legacy of a penny-pinching life dedicated to repaying him the only way she knew for cheating him of normality.

Based on the memory of a childhood visit with his special school when he was fourteen — the first time he had seen the sea — Charlton had put nearly all his legacy into buying his own home in Porthennis. He now survived on odd jobs for residents, casual employment in the tourist business during the summer and occasional wins on dogs and horses. His wardrobe was from jumble sales or charity shops and he scrounged more food than he bought. It was a miserable, demeaning existence, but better than being chased round a sawdust ring in wobbling, delirious mock panic before falling into a bowl of sticky paste, hysterical glee at his humiliation loud in his ears.

But now — automatic lust at the girl in the picture was replaced with a glitter of anticipation in his eyes — now he had a chance to make people who patronised him out of pity squirm and obey. He knew there was something, all he needed was the details. He had not been able to trick the information out of Martha Shaw, but there were others who must know. One of them, he was certain, would let it slip. Meanwhile he had to continue as the grateful menial, waiting for his chance to make others dance to his tune. Charlton finished his breakfast and tossed the plastic cereal bowl into the sink. Driving his invalid car out of Porthennis towards Penzance and his summer job operating the roundabout at a travelling fair, he wondered what conclusion the police had reached over Martha Shaw's death and whether Ruth Harvey would be home again by the time he returned in the evening.

Maltravers sat among tumbled rocks on Porthennis beach — there was scarcely enough sand around him to fill a bucket, let alone build a castle — throwing pebbles at a target of stones he had set up twenty feet away. Forearms on raised knees, Tess gazed across empty, crinkled cellophane sea buttered with sunlight. Voices of scattered holiday families floated in lazy morning quietness.

"Where the hell has he got to?" she demanded impatiently.

"God knows." Maltravers's arm hurled forward and a stone ricocheted among boulders like a steel ball in a pinball machine. "He must have gone out early, because I was up by seven." Another stone missed and bounced high in bright, languid air before rattling into a crevice. "But he seems to enjoy playing the man of mystery."

"Don't be stupid!" Tess's voice was sharp with rejection. "He wasn't like that. He was absolutely serious, and very unhappy about it."

Maltravers abandoned his target practice. "All right, calm down. But friend Mortimer has left too many loose ends hanging. I can accept he picked up your thoughts last night — I've come across stranger things than that which can't be explained in this life — but what has Martha Shaw's death got to do with us?"

"Martha Shaw's murder," Tess corrected. "I believed him when he said that, and you would as well if you'd been there."

"And you believe we're going to become mixed up in it in some way?"

Tess looked at the sea again for a few moments. "Frankly, yes. But it would help if he could tell us how."

"Then it would help if he reappeared." Maltravers lobbed a larger stone across the rocks and his target tumbled noisily. He had gone to Lacey's cottage earlier that morning, but there had been no reply. Passing time on the beach while Helen drove into Penzance to do her weekly shopping was becoming frustrating.

"Perhaps he's back now," Tess suggested. "We've been down here more than an hour."

As they left, they passed a concrete reservoir built into the beach, refilled twice a day by the tide to leave a shallow pool of clear water. Children were sailing toy boats or hurling sparkling bead curtains of water over each other with waving arms as parents watched. One woman nudged her husband and said something as she indicated Tess; it was her daughter who had been sick during the previous afternoon's matinée. The man looked up from his newspaper, then shook his head disbelievingly. More people were arriving, excited, chattering family safaris equipped with new shrimping nets, inflatable dinghies, woven raffia beach mats, dogs and transistor radios. An unremarkable Saturday morning in a Cornish holiday village, where visitors had been animated by news of a local sculptor killed when a statue fell on her; something more interesting than the weather to mention on picture postcards home.

Helen had returned but Lacey had not, and she suggested they asked round the harbour if anyone had seen him; his continuing absence was becoming unbearable. His eerie awareness — and now his disappearance after promising he would talk to Maltravers — had transformed him from the intriguing into something sinister.

It was less busy as they walked along the harbour front; Saturday was changeover day when many holidaymakers left in the morning to be replaced by new ones in the afternoon. While Maltravers was buying an *Independent* in the newsagents, Helen spoke to a couple of villagers, but neither had seen Lacey. As they stood outside the general store, Dorothy Lowe came out and saw them.

"Heard about Belvedere?" she asked before Helen could speak, booming contralto voice gloomy with satisfaction. "Silly bugger fell down his own steps on his way home last night. Out of his tree, of course. Hardly able to stand up straight when I left the Steamer at closing time."

Helen looked dismayed. "How is he?"

"Alive." Dorothy almost sounded disappointed. "Nothing worse than a crack on the back of his thick head. His dignity would be dented if he had any left."

"Sympathetic soul," Maltravers murmured to Tess.

"Is he in hospital?" Helen asked.

"Of course he isn't. They took him there about midnight after someone found him, but he discharged himself as soon as they'd patched him up." She indicated her basket of groceries. "First thing this morning he's ringing me up asking for iron rations."

She snorted impatiently. "He'll expect us all to wait on him hand and foot like the Great Panjandrum. Probably want one of us to finish off some of his work for him. Don't bother visiting. He's in an even fouler mood than usual."

"And what about Ruth?" Helen added. "We've heard what happened to Martha. She's staying with you isn't she?"

"Only for the time being. Wants to go home. Still in a state of shock of course." Dorothy's weather-beaten moon face shivered. "Must have been awful finding her like that. Can't have felt a thing though. Ruth came to me as soon as the police brought her back. Keeps going on about Martha not having been given the last rites, as if that mattered."

"But what are the police doing?" Helen added.

"Wasting their time with a lot of damn fool questions," Dorothy replied impatiently. "When I first saw Martha working on that stone, I told her she was mad not to put some supports round it. Probably thought that God would look after her. Anyway, I'd better get back with this lot. Goodbye."

As the old woman — who had ignored Maltravers and Tess — stalked away up the street by the clock tower, Helen called after her.

"Dorothy! Have you seen Mortimer anywhere?"

"Mortimer?" She turned back. "Yes. He was driving off when I was walking the dog first thing. About half past six."

"Where was he going?"

"Didn't stop to tell me. Didn't even wave back. Seemed in a hurry." Having given the information, she resumed up the hill. "Going towards Penzance," she called without looking round again.

"Who's she?" Maltravers asked.

"Dorothy Lowe," Helen replied. "Sorry, I should have introduced you. Another of the School. Belvedere said last night she'd taken Ruth in."

Maltravers looked after the retreating figure. "Is callousness written into their constitution? One old friend killed, another obviously distressed and Belvedere nearly breaking his neck. What does it take to make her show some sympathy?"

"They're all like that," Helen replied. "They insult each other as casually as they insult everyone else. It's all part of the act. Anyway, let's see if anyone in the Steamer knows where Mortimer's got to."

Wide open doors and windows had dispersed the concentrated smog of tobacco smoke and beer fumes laid down the previous evening. There were few people inside, one couple taking an early lunch of traditional star-gazy pie, heads of cooked pilchards poking through the crust, staring at the diners reproachfully. Jack Bocastle, the landlord, had not seen Lacey, then scowled when Helen mentioned Belvedere.

"Set new bench marks last night," he replied. "In drink and bloody bad manners. Some Yank believed everything he said — he even threw in the one about getting Greta Garbo to show him her tits — and bought him half a bottle of rum. Without my knowledge, or I'd have put a stop to it sharpish. Next thing he's trying to touch up the ladies until me and a couple of the lads told him to behave. He quietened down after that."

"How was he when he left?" Maltravers asked.

"Paralytic." Bocastle slurped coffee through an ornate Edwardian moustache, wiping away the remains and drying his hand on a bar cloth. "And he was in a funny old mood in the last half hour."

"Funny? How?"

"Maudlin." Bocastle indicated where a polished brass ship's propeller stood on the end of the bar against the wall. "Sat over there, mumbling to himself. When I threw him out — he'd still be here if I hadn't — he started going on about someone called Nancy. Grabbed hold of me at the door shouting 'Wasn't my fault!' I told him if he didn't pipe down I'd call Mike Nicholls and he could sober up in the cells. Then he went."

"Who's Nancy?" Maltravers looked enquiringly from the landlord to Helen, but both shook their heads.

Bocastle shrugged. "Probably some bird he got in the club fifty years ago. Excuse me." He left them to serve more customers.

"Definitely a drinker's drinker our Belvedere," Maltravers remarked. "He was lucky not to hurt himself more than he did."

"He could have been killed," Helen told him. "Those steps up to his cottage are horrendous. I bet he's in here again tonight though. They'll have to nail him in a box to stop him."

"I wonder who Nancy was?" Maltravers looked thoughtful. "It sounds as though he was upset about her, which is not the sort of reaction I'd expect from Belvedere under any circumstances."

"I've never heard of her," Helen said. "Given half a chance, they bore you stiff with nostalgia about all the ones who've come and gone and I'm certain that name's never come up."

Tess glanced at the clock behind the bar. "Even allowing for that being fast, I've got to go to work. You won't need the car will you?"

"I've no intention of leaving until our wandering mystic returns," Maltravers said. "Then I'm going to pin him to a chair and find out exactly what he's talking about."

Tess slid off the bar-stool. "Tread softly. He's a walking landmine."

Maltravers and Helen ordered lunch, and, as they waited for their food, she went to ask some other locals about Lacey. Maltravers opened the *Independent*, which had a front page paragraph reporting Martha Shaw's death with a cross-reference to an obituary inside.

G K Chesterton once said that journalism consists of telling people Lord Jones is dead when they had been unaware he was alive in the first place. The obituaries included a civil servant who had spent his entire career hidden from public gaze in Whitehall, the next for a woman with an unpronounceable Polish name, her contribution to Western literature as unreadable as it was forgotten, followed by a racing driver, fleeting success thirty years ago earning his seven brief sentences. Martha Shaw had done rather better and even merited a picture.

The sudden death of sculptress Martha Elisabeth Shaw ends a career which began as a disciple of Henry Moore and finished with a reputation blossoming too late.

Born in Uppingham, where her father was assistant art master at the public school, Martha Shaw showed early promise as a portrait painter before turning to sculpture under Moore's influence, although her early work was too derivative of the master to have any status of its own.

After living in France between the wars, she moved to Porthennis in Cornwall shortly after the Second World War, becoming one of the self-styled and frequently self-indulgent artists' School which flourished there until the 1960s. The painter Frank Morgan, the only one to enjoy any reputation (although the fallen idol Belvedere Scott was also a member), became her mentor, guiding her towards a style which owed little or nothing to previous influences.

Throughout most of her life, commissions were scarce and only Morgan's support enabled her to keep working. But in recent years she was tardily recognised as arguably comparable to Hepworth and worthy of a significant, if minor, place in late twentieth century art.

A passionate Communist in her youth — although perhaps more by association than conviction; the philosophy was embraced by several members of the Porthennis School — Martha Shaw was also a lifelong atheist until her conversion to Roman Catholicism almost at the end. It will be a savage irony if, as first reports indicate, she died when a statue of the Virgin and Child she was completing for Westminster Cathedral fell on her while she was working.

Helen rejoined Maltravers as he finished reading. "No Mortimer?"

"No. There's apparently been no sign of him since Dorothy saw him this morning. Heaven knows where he is."

"Tell me more about the School," he said. "I've met Belvedere and Dorothy and I know about Martha and Ruth. Anyone else left?"

"Edward Cunningham, who was also a sculptor but now makes pottery because there's more money in it, Edith Hallam-West, who's a calligrapher but better known as a wildlife artist, and Patrick Dawson," Helen said. "Patrick's the most interesting. He paints very bleak and lonely pictures of beaches with enigmatic figures. They don't sell well because most people find them depressing, but they're good and I rather like them. I've got one at the cottage."

"So there's . . ." Maltravers counted rapidly. "One, two three . . . six still around and Martha was alive and working up to yesterday? They should bottle the air round here and sell it."

"They're indestructible," Helen said. "Martha's only the fourth of what are regarded as the originals to die. The others were Morgan, Jonathan Bright — and he was turned seventy when he finally went a couple of years ago — and Agnes Thorpe of course."

"Agnes who built the Botallack? I didn't realise she was part of it."

"It happened because of her," Helen explained. "Belvedere and Dorothy were the first to arrive after the war to help build the theatre."

"Incidentally, you did say they were lovers didn't you?" Maltravers put in. "From her reaction just now they're not singing love's old sweet song. She obviously detests him."

"I don't think they ever really loved each other," Helen said. "Not properly. In the early days Dorothy had as many men as Belvedere had women. They even rebelled against each other. Anyway, that's how the School started and the others drifted in over the next few years. They were a sort of commune, fighting the philistines. They wanted to establish Porthennis as a great cultural centre with its own theatre and art galleries and God knows what else. Quite mad of course. Before the roads improved and everybody had cars, this place was beyond nowhere."

"And what happened to Agnes? She didn't make it to ripe old age."

"Ah, the Porthennis mystery. You haven't walked the coast path to Morsylla yet have you?"

"No. Tess and I were planning to go tomorrow when she's free."

"Look at this." Helen led him to a framed tidal map of Mounts Bay on one wall. Her finger traced pecked lines of a footpath along the cliff edge. "There are coombes through the undergrowth to the beach and . . ." She indicated one spot. "Just here it was, Cat's Head cove below the old coastguard lookout. Agnes was fanatical about keeping fit and went swimming there alone every evening in the summer. One night in 1951 she didn't come back and they found her clothes and towel on the rocks."

"Drowned?"

"That's what everyone thought of course, but her body was never washed up." Helen momentarily switched into mock-Cornish. "And the bay always gives up its dead, moi dear. That's

42

not strictly true, because a few years back a fishing boat went down and they never found any of the crew, but given the sea conditions and where she went in, there was no reason at all why Agnes shouldn't have come ashore. According to the tides, she should have been found less than a mile along the coast. But she wasn't . . . Then the suicide note turned up."

"Did it indeed? Who found it?"

"One of the other members of the School, I can't remember which," Helen replied. "It said she'd been told she had cancer and couldn't face it. After a while, her death was presumed even without a body and there was an inquest. Dorothy and Belvedere and some of the others said she'd been depressed but wouldn't tell them why. The coroner had no option but to say she took her own life."

Bocastle called from the bar with their meal and they took their plates to one of the tables.

"And her body was never found?" Maltravers confirmed as he began to spread pâté on his toast.

"No." Helen raised an eyebrow. "And neither was the doctor who'd told her she had cancer. Her regular one said she hadn't been to see him for months and it wasn't anyone else local. There weren't many around in those days and they were all checked."

"Perhaps she'd gone to one in London?" Maltravers suggested.

"Possibly," Helen acknowledged. "But why? You don't suddenly decide you think you've got cancer and dash off to a doctor three hundred miles away to confirm it. You go to your local one."

"I see the mystery," Maltravers agreed. "How do you know so much about it?"

"It's all in the guidebooks and Belvedere and the others still go to the beach on the anniversary for a minute's silence. No prayers or anything, they all gave up any religious beliefs years ago."

Maltravers found the image of ageing artists standing by the evening sea in memory of a woman who died nearly forty years earlier bizarre. Encounters with Scott and Dorothy Lowe had indicated little sentiment among their emotions; they both appeared to relish their roles as outrageous elderly Bohemians and the rest were presumably the same. A solemn annual ceremony of mourning appeared totally out of character.

"Except for Martha. Her obit says she'd become a Catholic."

"Yes, and that went down like a fart in church," Helen said. "She went to Rome to look at art and said God spoke to her in St Peter's."

Maltravers grinned. "That must have made her popular."

"Belvedere told her she must have been drunk, but it's not funny. They've grown old together and stopped having new ideas years ago. There was a row in here one night you wouldn't believe. Jack Bocastle stepped in just in time to stop Dorothy hitting Martha with a bottle and the others were all taking Dorothy's side." Helen shuddered off the memory. "It was grotesque. A bunch of pensioners fighting like lager louts."

"Just because Martha had got religion?" Maltravers shook his head. "And yet each year they stand on the beach and remember Agnes Thorpe? That's . . . disproportionate. Correction. That's insane."

"I sometimes think they are insane." Helen glanced round the Steamer. "In winter this place is like the old days. There are incredible wild seas crashing over the harbour wall and we sit in here at night listening to the wind. There are no tourists, and it's just a Cornish fishing village again. That's when you see them as they really are."

Maltravers frowned as he caught the note in her voice. "Which is?"

Helen looked into her glass for a moment. "Old. Bitter. Resentful. Slightly pitiful. Missing their summer audience of tourists." She looked up at him. "And secretive. They cling on to certain things. It's as though they're all members of a select society and the rest of us are outside a charmed circle. Even those who've lived here all their lives."

"Memories of how it began may be all they've got left," Maltravers remarked. "Their dreams didn't come true, but they were the only people who shared them. I can believe they'd guard them jealously."

"Come back in winter and see what you think then." Helen shook her head. "I know what you mean, but if that's all it was to it, they'd just be rather sad. It's more as if they are . . ." She paused, seeking an elusive word.

"Obsessed, Helen?"

Maltravers looked up at the figure who had silently appeared beside their table. "Hello, Mortimer. Where the hell have you been?"

Chapter Four

"What's this muck?" Scott's fork suspiciously probed a small mound of cottage cheese set on lettuce leaves between two tomatoes; it bore a marked resemblance to a banal serving suggestion illustration on the side of the tin. "It's bloody vegetarian, isn't it?"

"Vegetarian, yes. Bloody, no," Dorothy Lowe told him crossly. "It'll do you more good than your usual diet of alcohol and instant curries. Do you know how many packets there are in your pantry?"

He thrust the tray away across his bed. He was dressed in a grubby, creased nightshirt, lines across his battered face deepened by pain and weariness.

"At least they've got some meat in them. Chuck one in a pan. It only takes ten minutes."

"Cook it yourself," Dorothy snapped. "I've already spent nearly two hours running around after you. You're not going to take any notice of what the doctor said about staying in bed, are you?"

"You die if you stay in bed. And I don't want to die." He glared at Dorothy challengingly. "Do you want to? Die?"

"We're all going to die one day. It doesn't matter."

"Mattie thought it did. Said we'd all roast in eternal flames or some crap like that."

Dorothy looked out of the bedroom window across the wilderness that was Scott's garden. "We told her what we thought of that. She'd become more Catholic than the Pope."

Scott winced as he turned his head towards her. "Let's face it

46

Dottie, none of us is weeping over her." He laughed sourly. "Blessing in disguise."

"After all these years," Dorothy suddenly sounded very sad. "It's not ending the way we planned is it?"

"I've forgotten what we planned now."

"I haven't."

She remained with her back to him; his mockery at her tears would have been unbearable. Memories swelled inside her, fired by betrayed hopes, acid with remembered pain, vivid with lost passion. The young could never comprehend that the very old could once have been like them, with eager bodies and driven by the importance of fierce ideals, however irrational. And not all the old become resigned and philosophical. She wanted to get away from Belvedere and nurse her feelings alone.

"How did you manage to fall over anyway?" she asked as she crossed to the bedroom door. "I've known you get up those steps with enough inside you to fell an ox."

"Must have slipped," he mumbled. "Could have happened to anyone."

"You're getting senile."

"We're all getting senile." He leered at her. "Admit it, Dottie. How long since you've had a good rogering?"

"Not as long as you!"

For a moment they glared at each other; their combined ages were a hundred and fifty-nine. They had first met when she was eighteen and he was thirty-one and their relationship had been as fiery as the French Pyrenean sun under which they had made love. After more than half a century, love had crumbled through fading affection and indifference to casual contempt. Images of strong naked bodies, twined excitedly together and panting with ecstasy were faded and dead as sepia photographs. Simultaneously, each lost the courage to meet the other's eyes.

"If you're well enough to think about fornicating, you're well enough to look after yourself, you bloody old goat!" The door slammed.

Scott shouted an obscenity, then yelped as bruised flesh and strained muscles shot pain through him. Sparse, stringy hair at

47

the base of his skull had been shaved off and a wide strip of sticking plaster covered the stitches holding split skin together. The tray slid to the floor, contents spilling over the carpet. He swore again, then cautiously moved his legs off the brass bed. Clutching furniture, he hobbled to where his clothes lay on a chair and awkwardly began to dress.

"Bloody doctors. Bloody nurses. Bloody Dottie."

The litany continued as he pulled on a shirt and struggled with his trousers. He had been a difficult casualty patient, sobered by his fall, aggressively threatening physical violence to anyone who approached with a hypodermic. A muscular sister had been hurled across the room when she tried a brisk "Come along, Mr Scott, let's stop being silly and do as we're told, shall we?" tactic. Having established that there appeared to be nothing broken, a house surgeon had finally allowed him to leave only after he had made it quite clear in front of witnesses that the hospital could accept no responsibility if he insisted on discharging himself. When Social Services had been advised, they had been amused. Home visits by community nurses a few years earlier, after Scott's doctor had reported he was suffering from flu, recorded that one girl had said if he was that randy when he was ill, she would not go near him when he was better without an armed guard.

Downstairs, Scott drank half a tumbler of rum and felt better. He could eat in the Steamer later; his injuries should ensure ample sympathetic drinks. He went into his front room, where a wide window faced down the hill across falling rooftops of lower houses to the sea. The point where he had fallen was just visible before the steps curved out of sight. For a long time he looked at the spot.

"Who the hell were you?" he muttered.

Ruth Harvey pulled the door open the instant Dorothy inserted her key. Eyes full of panic, she resembled a startled bird. She was wearing one of her endless collection of printed floral frocks, garish colours exaggerating chalky face beneath white hair tied back in a bun and held in a rubber band. She had gone grey almost overnight when she was twenty-six.

"It's the police!" she gasped. "They want to go into Martha's studio again."

"Then why didn't you take them?" Dorothy snapped.

"They've only just arrived." Thin hands fluttered helplessly. "I wanted you to be here. I knew I'd get confused when they started asking more questions and —"

"Oh, for God's sake!" Dorothy slammed her basket down on the hall table. "Where are they?"

"In the front room. I told them you wouldn't be long."

The two men stood up as Dorothy entered the room; they appeared relieved to see her.

"Hello, Miss Lowe. Detective Sergeant Doughty. It's in connection with Miss Shaw's death."

"I didn't imagine it was a social call." Dorothy glared impatiently at Ruth, silently ordering her to hide her nervousness. "Your people wouldn't let me in yesterday."

"It wasn't possible at the time," Doughty replied evenly. "However, we want to take Miss Harvey into the studio again and she asked if you could be there as well. We have no objections."

He smiled reassuringly at Ruth. "There's nothing to worry about. We just want to check a few details."

"Will it take long?" Dorothy demanded.

"I don't imagine so. You don't have to be there."

Dorothy looked at Ruth's pleading face and sighed. "Yes I do."

As they approached the studio, Ruth became increasingly agitated and only a warning look from Dorothy kept her under control. The door was secured by a padlock the police had fitted. Doughty unfastened it and turned on the lights. Nearly six feet long, the uncompleted statue lay across the floor; it had taken levers and the combined strength of five men to lift it off Martha Shaw's body. Once the police photographer and forensic team had finished, someone had considerately washed off blood and crushed flesh embedded with splinters of bone. One end tapered into the outline of bare feet beneath the hem of a robe emerging out of the rock. Doughty squinted up at the skylight, broken glass of four of its six frames replaced with hardboard.

"It was lowered in through there by crane," he confirmed.

"Martha had her studio built next to the road for that very reason." Dorothy sounded impatient.

Doughty walked round the piece of granite, assessing its shape and probable weight. "I assume this is the bottom?" He indicated the half-sculpted feet.

"Naturally," said Dorothy. "That's where the feet usually go."

"But that would mean it was top heavy when it was standing up," Doughty remarked.

"Statues always are," Dorothy told him. "The human body is. Those damned angels you see in churchyards only stay upright because they're fixed at the base."

"But why did she start work at the bottom?" Doughty persisted. "Surely it would have been safer —"

"Sergeant," Dorothy interrupted impatiently, "if artists always did things the safe way, Michelangelo would have painted panels on the ground and had them nailed on the ceiling of the Sistine Chapel by workmen. Logic has nothing to do with where an artist starts work."

"But why wasn't it propped up?"

"Don't think we didn't suggest it to her. She kept saying she would, but never got around to it."

Turning his attention from the statue, Doughty crossed to where the stepladder had been propped against a wall. The metal was chipped and flecked with rust and three of the wooden steps had retaining screws missing. He lifted one up and let it fall again.

"If this was in a factory, a Public Health Inspector would have taken out a prosecution," he commented.

"This isn't the shopfloor at Fords," Dorothy replied sharply. "It's an artist's studio. Health and safety regulations have nothing to do with it."

"Miss Shaw might still be alive if they did."

Ruth Harvey suddenly sobbed and ran out of the studio.

"Oh, well done," Dorothy said sarcastically. "Very diplomatic. Have you quite finished now?"

"For the time being," Doughty agreed cautiously. "Although we may have to come back if my inspector thinks it's necessary."

"Well next time, ask for me. Miss Harvey's in a bad enough state as it is."

"I'm sorry to have distressed her." Doughty looked at Dorothy. "You know more about this sort of thing than I do, Miss Lowe. What do you think happened?"

"I would have thought it was obvious. Martha was standing on the ladder starting work on the top. You can see the first chisel marks. The ladder must have gone off balance and she grabbed at the statue and pulled it down on her. Of course, I'm not a policeman. Heaven knows what you people think."

There was a silence as she waited for a reply that did not come.

"Is that all, then?" she demanded and when Doughty nodded, she marched out, the CID in her wake. She watched them walk down Fern Hill towards their car. As they vanished, she crossed the garden into the cottage where Ruth was sitting in the front room staring at a photograph on the sideboard of Martha and herself, laughing on the rocks of Land's End thirty years earlier, arms around each other.

"It's all right, they've gone." Dorothy was gruffly sympathetic. "Sorry it upset you."

Ruth did not move or look at her as she began to weep silently again.

"So what have we got?" Detective Inspector Brian Emsley tossed the initial report into Martha Shaw's death on to his desk. "Miss Lowe could be quite right. It has all the signs of an accident."

"Looks that way," Doughty agreed. "But somebody could have gone in there and pushed it."

"Who?" demanded Emsley sharply. "And why?"

"Don't know," Doughty admitted. "But there are places to hide in that studio. Someone could have done it, then waited until Ruth Harvey and Charlton went to call us before making off. But there's no smell of a motive. Miss Shaw's solicitor says she left everything to the Little Sisters of Mercy, apart from the house which is Miss Harvey's, but only for her lifetime. She'll have to manage on her old age pension and any savings she's got."

"I can't see the Little Sisters of Mercy bumping her off," Emsley commented. "And Miss Harvey hardly counts as a major beneficiary. Anyway, I thought they were in love with each other."

"There's no way Ruth Harvey did it." Doughty sounded positive. "She's genuinely grief-stricken."

"And Miss Shaw's closest friends are those geriatric Porthennis artists." Emsley thought for a moment, then shook his head. "Mad as hatters of course, but I can't really see any of them as a murderer. What reason would any of them have?"

"There'd apparently been a big row between them and Martha Shaw," Doughty pointed out. "They objected to her becoming a Catholic."

"They used to burn people at the stake for things like that," Emsley admitted. "Perhaps they still do in Tehran, but not in Cornwall."

He looked up at Doughty. "Could there be anyone else?"

"Not that we can see," Doughty replied. "I've talked to Mike Nicholls, the neighbourhood PC, who knows just about everyone and everything in Porthennis. All the villagers knew Martha Shaw of course — it's that sort of place — but apart from her artistic friends there was nobody special."

"What about a visitor? The place is full of them."

"And we'd have a hell of a job tracing them all," Doughty pointed out. "Most of them rent cottages for a fortnight then disappear or just make day trips from somewhere else. Anyway, why should one of them suddenly decide to kill a harmless old woman? There's no sign of theft."

"Nutty rapist covering his tracks?" Emsley suggested.

"The lower part of her body wasn't crushed and the medical report says there are no indications of sexual attack," Doughty replied. "It looks a total non-starter."

"Just covering all the options." Emsley pushed the report across the desk. "Keep at it and let me know if anything turns up, but at the moment my money's on accidental death. We've got more urgent things with that armed bank raid. Now the security guard's dead, that's certainly a murder hunt. We haven't got time to waste looking for killers who probably don't exist."

Suspended from barley sugar twisted poles, painted wooden horses with teeth carved in rigid mock smiles rose and fell in an endless circular chase. Children waved to their parents each time they reached them, shouts of greeting mingling with deafening amplified pop music. In the control box at the carousel's centre, Charlton sat on a wooden chair, a pile of newspapers raising him sufficiently to see outside. He waited for the two teenage girls to pass his kaleidoscope view again, young flesh firm and sun-pink in shorts and sleeveless cotton shirts. They would casually give their bodies to any man who took their fancy; any normal man. Charlton had to pay for such pleasures, and it was a long time since he had been able to afford them.

The girls flashed by and Charlton absently reached for the switch to stop the roundabout. Ruth Harvey was the answer now. In her distress she would talk with increasing carelessness as he coaxed and tricked her. Charlton had never experienced the taste of power over others and the prospect excited him with its promise and its possibilities.

Unlike Helen's cottage, the two downstairs rooms in Lacey's remained separate. Sunshine poured through the front window, shining off lemon Regency stripe paper and gleaming on yellow cane furniture. Maltravers examined autographed photographs on the mantelpiece of icons of the sixties — Dusty Springfield, Julie Christie, Jean Shrimpton — who had worn Lacey creations. A group picture at a party showed a younger Lacey, flamboyant in velvet jacket and ruffled silk shirt, surrounded by faces now only half remembered, but which had once dominated popular culture.

"It was the best of times to be young, but I have to remind myself now that it all happened," Lacey remarked. "Where did they all go?"

"Why did you come here?" Maltravers asked. "Porthennis is a long way from Carnaby Street."

"I saw the writing on the wall," he replied. "I cringe when I see some of them today, wrinklies like me trying to pretend it never ended. And old footage on television looks as quaint as the twenties now."

Maltravers and Helen sat on a bamboo settee with Beardsley-style patterned cushions and Lacey stood with his back to the window.

"I refuse to become nostalgic," he added. "There's no bore like a sixties bore. And there are more important things to talk about."

"Yes there are," Maltravers replied. "And a lot of questions. I find you . . . worrying, Mortimer."

Lacey laughed. "You're not the first."

"I can believe it. What you said to Tess last night was true, but that's a closed book and I won't talk about it. But if you were right about that, I've got to accept you could be right about Martha Shaw being murdered."

"I had to convince you," Lacey told him simply.

"Then why can't you tell us who did it? You read Tess's mind at the Botallack, why can't you lock on to the killer?"

"Don't overestimate me," Lacey replied. "Most of the time people guard their thoughts. When you talk to somebody, you're at least subconsciously aware of what you're saying, how they are reacting to it, why you're saying certain things. Absolute, pure thought without any defences around it is very rare. Tess did it during the play for just one moment of immense concentration. For a few seconds, there was nothing in her mind but the essential images and emotions of a single real incident. I could count on one hand the number of times I've known that happen."

Maltravers leaned forward, elbows resting on his knees, mouth against fingertips of touching palms, and thought for a few moments.

"All right." He straightened up again. "But if you can do that — and know the moment Martha Shaw died when you were standing in this room — you can do other things. Like point us in a few directions."

"How about to the police?" Helen suggested.

"The police don't have a great deal of time for people claiming inexplicable second sense," Lacey remarked. "I have no wish to change my reputation from Porthennis eccentric into local loony. However, if we find definite evidence, then we certainly go to them."

"You also told Tess that she and I — and Helen — would become involved in Martha Shaw's death," Maltravers added. "Enlarge."

"That's difficult. I'm certain of it, but can't explain how."

"Very runic. Did the Cornish pixies tell you?"

"Don't disappoint me, Gus," Lacey replied levelly. "You're too intelligent to mock this. If you weren't, you'd have told me I was out of my mind at the start and we wouldn't be having this conversation."

Maltravers shrugged. "You can't blame me for trying to give things a touch of normality. Tess and I came down to Cornwall because of her job — extravagant though acting can be, that's what it is — stay with Helen and give me time to do some writing. We didn't anticipate running into sudden death and a man who would once have been hanged for witchcraft."

"Porthennis may have other things you didn't expect," Lacey told him. "I'm afraid can't explain that either."

"If I insisted on explanations all along the line, we'd get nowhere." Maltravers stood up. "So where do we start? How about with your trip this morning? You said you had a compulsion to visit a church?"

"Yes, but not any one. I knew it wasn't here or even in Penzance."

"So how did you find it?"

"I kept driving until I felt I was getting near."

"Sounds like getting warm when you're playing hunt the slipper." Maltravers held his hand up in apology. "Sorry, but comments like that help my sense of proportion. Where did you end up?"

"A Roman Catholic church in Wenlock," Lacey replied. "Nearly fifty miles away. As soon as I stopped outside I knew it was the right place. Don't ask how. I went inside and sat there.

After a while the priest came and asked if he could help me, but I just said I wanted to pray. The trouble is, I'm not a Catholic and was worried I'd make some mistake of procedure and he'd be calling the police accusing me of planning to steal the altar cross."

"The way of the mystic was ever hard," Maltravers commented. "So what happened?"

"I felt Martha's presence, there are no arguments about that. But I didn't know why."

"Did she ever worship there?"

"She may have done," Lacey replied. "She could have gone to any Catholic church for all I know. But her regular one was Our Lady Immaculate in Penzance."

"You're sure of that?"

"Positive. I gave her a lift there one Sunday when her car was out of action and I happened to be going that way."

Maltravers thought for a moment. "So if her . . . spirit, shall we say, was trying to tell you something, that's where it's most likely to have been. With the BVM in Penzance."

"I've never claimed powers of communication with the dead," Lacey corrected. "That's a different gift to mine. All I know is Martha had been in that church and something happened there which was important."

"Did you speak to the priest again before you left?"

"Yes. I said a friend from Porthennis had been to his church and asked if he remembered her. He knew nobody from this area."

"Perhaps she didn't see the priest," said Maltravers. "She could have just gone there for some reason . . . but why travel fifty miles when her own church is only ten minutes' drive away?"

"I'm afraid I'm rather better at unearthing problems than supplying answers," Lacey apologised. "I only know that something took me to that particular church."

"Unfortunately, the only spirit that moves me comes in a bottle and is served with ice and tonic," Maltravers said. "And it doesn't tend to help me think clearly. So what do you suggest we do?"

"Specifically, nothing."

Maltravers raised his eyebrows. "Nothing? Just sit around until the answers find us? Hang around in the Steamer for a convenient guilty confession? Stumble across clues by way of serendipity? Wait for something to turn up? Mr Micawber tried that and ended up in Australia."

"Things will turn up," Lacey assured him. "Things will happen. What we have to do is recognise and interpret them." He suddenly appeared uncomfortable as he turned away and looked through the window. "I can appreciate you joking, Gus, but I don't think any of us will be laughing when this is finished. There's evil somewhere out there."

"Evil?" Maltravers weighed the word as he repeated it. Even from Lacey it seemed melodramatic. "What are you trying to do now, Mortimer? Scare me?"

"No. I'm trying to warn you."

Maltravers scowled at him, wishing he had not sounded so serious.

Chapter Five

Patrick Dawson's bony, stained fingers juggled shreds of tobacco and a thin strip of paper with the automatic skill of more than sixty years; he had started smoking when he was nine. The paper was twisted into an irregular tube, tongue flashed along its gummed edge with lizard speed. Fragments of shredded leaf protruding from one end were pinched away and the tube was smoothed out, slipped between his lips and lit from a battered, gunmetal petrol lighter's bulging flame with the speed of a conjuror. Dark-grey, humourless eyes in a long hollow face blotched with patches of seaweed brown, remained fixed on his canvas. He dropped the lighter into the pocket of a paint-spattered cream linen jacket and picked up his brush again, carefully deepening the colour beneath a falling wave. Drooping from the centre of a wide mouth turned down at pointed ends, the cigarette rose and fell as he spoke.

"Are the police satisfied it was an accident?" Faint but indelible echoes of Lancashire speech from a Salford childhood were overlaid with cadences picked up in the Merchant Navy and nearly half a lifetime in Porthennis. He did not look away from his work as he asked the question.

"I think so."

"But if it wasn't . . ." The voice was only half-attentive as he became absorbed in correcting details. Worn canvas on the back of his chair strained as he leaned back. "You think someone pushed it?"

"They could have, couldn't they?"

The suggestion had no immediate effect; Dawson had other things on his mind. That wave was right, but that shadow . . .

58

"For God's sake, Patrick, leave it alone! Did you hear what I said?"

Dawson's head revolved slowly and he looked straight at Ruth Harvey, standing by the far wall of his studio. Behind her hung a large beach scene, wilderness sand and dark, menacing sea with a small solitary figure — it was impossible to say if it was man or woman — sitting in isolation and gazing into emptiness.

"I heard." Having briefly given direct attention, his preoccupation with the shadow of the rocks returned.

"And?" she demanded.

"And what?"

"Who was it?"

"Who says it was anybody? Apart from you."

"Nobody's saying it. But they could be thinking it."

Smoke weaved up between thin nostrils and Dawson squinted as his eyes watered. "I'm not thinking it, Ruth."

"Aren't you?"

Dawson replaced the paintbrush in the handful he was holding and selected another, working it into his palette. "It was an accident."

"Then it was a very convenient one, wasn't it?" Her voice choked with sobs as she lost control.

Dawson paused as he attended to the shadow, then turned to her again. "These things happen, Ruth. What do the others think?"

"You're the first I've talked to."

"They'll say the same. You'll see."

Ruth twisted the eternity ring on her finger helplessly. She had needed to get her heart very high for this visit, overcoming crushing grief and a sense of terror with a determination to know, however awful knowing might be. And Dawson, as always, had been unmoved and immovable. She had never known anyone so unsympathetic to other people's emotions, indifferent because he did not share and could not comprehend them. But there was one thing; she had never known him to lie.

"Patrick, you've got to tell me," she said timidly. "Was it you?"

"No." The simple denial was not amplified and he did not even look up from his work again. Ruth accepted it without a word, then walked to the door, pausing as Dawson called her name. When she looked back at him, he was still considering his painting.

"Sorry about Martha," he said. It was the only expression of sympathy he had offered her. She walked out and he heard her footsteps descending the staircase to his gallery and shop. With a delicacy unexpected in a man so obviously strong despite his age, he perfected the shadow. The cigarette had burned down so short that the heat scorched his lips. His eyes screwed up as he pushed his lips forward and carefully removed the stub between pinched fingers before treading it out on the floor and starting to roll another, critically examining what he had done.

"Let it go, Ruth," he murmured to himself. "Just let it go."

Tess left the Botallack shortly before midnight after a birthday party on the set for one of the cast. As she reached the top of Fern Hill, the streetlamps were out, but a white wax gibbous moon glittered in a blade of diamonds across placid, hammered silver sea gently washing the great open mouth of Mounts Bay. There was no other traffic, but she drove slowly, alert for creatures of the dark. Idly humming Desdemona's melancholy willow lament, she suddenly caught a glimpse of a figure which leapt out of the blaze of her headlights back into the shadow of hedges then there was a clump as though she had struck something. She stopped violently and twisted round in her seat, peering anxiously at the road behind her, flooded crimson by the glare of brake lights. There was no sign of anyone, injured or unharmed.

As she waited for someone to appear, the flashing images of the moment replayed themselves in her brain and she was half conscious that something had been wrong with them. There had been a furtive urgency about the figure's hasty movements, not the natural actions of a late-night walker surprised by an unexpected vehicle. If she had hit them, they should be visibly lying there; if not they should have stepped out of the hedge again. Whatever the case, she had to investigate.

Opening the glove compartment, she found a torch and swore resignedly when it didn't work; there were times when Maltravers's incompetence over the most basic practical matters ceased to be an amusing eccentricity. As she got out of the car, a drift of night-scented stock reached her in the stillness and the only sound was the crisp rustle of waves on the beach below. Eyes probing moon-cast gloom, she cautiously walked back up the hill, keeping her distance from the hedges. The figure had looked like a child, but she was apprehensive as she neared the spot where it had vanished. On the roadway lay a broken tree branch, the probable explanation for the impact sound as she had driven over it. Eyes never leaving the hedge, she stooped and picked it up then stood very still, ears straining for sounds, but there was nothing.

She realised she was outside Martha Shaw's garden; opposite her the white painted wooden walls of her studio dimly caught the moonlight. To her left the cottage was in darkness and she remembered Dorothy Lowe had said Ruth Harvey was staying with her; was some teenager taking advantage of its emptiness to break in? She jumped at the faint noise of someone or something moving slightly among the bushes.

"Who's that?" Her voice sounded disproportionately loud. "What are you doing?"

There was no reply. Senses heightened, she gripped the branch more tightly as she crossed the narrow road and cautiously opened a wooden gate leading to the studio. While confident of being able to look after herself — at least two previous boyfriends who would not take no for an answer had painfully discovered her skill in self-defence — summer-thick bushes offered too many hiding places from where she could be attacked from behind. The gate remained open as she stepped on to a concrete path, then there was a sudden scuffling and someone leapt out immediately beside and beneath her. A punch in the stomach sent her staggering into a looming hydrangea bush and she half saw a figure dash through the open gate. An instant attempt to stand up was stopped as she grunted in pain, gasping for breath and by the time she managed to reach the gate the road was empty in both directions. Instantly abandoning any ideas of a futile chase in the darkness, she concentrated on analysing impressions. The fleeing figure had not looked right. Small as a child, but with wrong movements, the clumsiness not adolescent but — her mind groped for the right word — distorted. She shivered. The incident had been more than frightening; there had been a sense of malevolence about it. She realised she was still holding the branch and hurled it away before hurrying back to the car.

Maltravers was still up watching a late-night film on television when she returned to Helen's cottage.

"What's happened to you?" He pointed at a tear in her slacks.

"It must have been when . . . Has Helen gone to bed?"

"No. She's still working in her studio at the back. Why?"

"I want to ask her if she knows a dwarf."

"A dwarf?" Maltravers looked surprised. "Sleepy, Grumpy, Happy, Bashful, Doc, Sneezy and . . . no, it's gone. However, I can name all the Magnificent Seven, including Brad Dexter who everyone forgets, but he wasn't a dwarf."

"This is serious," she said impatiently. "I've just been attacked."

"By a dwarf?"

"Yes . . . Well, I think it was a dwarf. I only got a glimpse of him."

Maltravers turned off the set with the electronic control.

"It's been a difficult enough afternoon with Mortimer," he warned her. "I may have trouble coping with maniac midgets. However, try me."

He poured a drink while she explained then sat opposite her in the club porter's seat.

"Are you sure? It wasn't just a teenager?"

"No," she insisted. "I was falling over and couldn't see properly in the dark, but his movements were all wrong. He was . . . waddling."

"And he just pushed you and ran? Or waddled."

"Yes." Tess sipped her Scotch. "And what was he doing there? He must have been breaking in to Martha Shaw's cottage."

"Did you check?"

"No. I just wanted to get back here."

"Sounds like a nasty opportunist thief," Maltravers remarked. "It's sick, but homes were looted in Lockerbie after the Pan-Am air crash."

"But how would he know Ruth wasn't still in the cottage?"

"We know she's staying with Dorothy Lowe and we're strangers," Maltravers pointed out. "In a place as small as Porthennis word gets around. But is there a resident dwarf?"

"Helen may know," said Tess. "Anyway, I gather Mortimer turned up after I left the Steamer. What did he have to say for himself?"

"Quite a lot and up to his usual standard."

Maltravers related the afternoon's conversation and they were discussing it when Helen reappeared through the kitchen, wiping paint from her hands on a cloth.

"We've got a dwarf all right," she confirmed when Tess asked her. "Nick Charlton. I expect I ought to feel sorry for him, but he's a slimy little toad. He's lived here for . . . I'm not sure, at least ten years. Keeps himself alive with odd jobs and summer work. Why?"

She pulled a face of distaste as Tess explained. "He was breaking into Martha's cottage? The bastard."

"That's only our assumption," Maltravers said. "But why else would he have been around there at this time of night? Where does he live?"

"Behind the harbour front," Helen told him. "There's no reason for him to be up Fern Hill."

"If it was him," Maltravers added. "I don't imagine dwarfs are thick on the ground round here, but the Cornish are descendants of pocket-sized Ancient Britons. It could just have been a small person."

"No way," Tess contradicted. "It was a dwarf, so it must have been this Nick Charlton."

"Will you tell the police?" Helen asked. "Apart from anything else, he did attack you."

"It's not worth the hassle. Anyway, I can't prove anything and . . ." Tess stopped and shook her head uncomfortably. "But it was nasty and, I don't know, spooky. Not just because it happened in the dark, but . . ."

She looked at them both helplessly, unable to explain her feelings.

"But because it felt evil?" Maltravers suggested quietly. Tess stared at him, startled that he had instantly touched the precise word she had been searching for. "I'm afraid we're back with Mortimer. If he's not gone to bed, I'll ask him in for a nightcap and another chat."

Twenty minutes later there was a long silence in the room as Tess finished repeating her experience. Lacey had dismissed Maltravers's apologies for disturbing him almost as if he had expected his arrival. He had asked no questions while Tess had been speaking, but his eyes had grown increasingly sombre as he had listened.

"By the pricking of my thumbs, something wicked this way comes?" Maltravers said softly as Tess finished.

"Yes it does." Lacey sounded slightly distant. "In Shake-speare's day they were much closer to truths people either don't understand or laugh at now. Very foolish of them."

"So Charlton is our source of evil?" Maltravers suggested.

"Perhaps . . ." Lacey's hands traced patterns of uncertainty in the air. "But don't jump to conclusions. I recognised Nick Charlton for what he is the moment I met him. He's spiteful and has a disturbing amount of hatred in him. He's certainly *capable* of evil, but up to now he's gone no further than mischief."

"Mischief?" Maltravers echoed. "That's what children get up to."

"That's how it's used now, but it's a degree of evil," Lacey replied. "Look it up in a dictionary. The point is, has something happened which has made him go the whole hog?"

"And how far's the whole hog?" Maltravers asked.

"I don't know, but it's within his nature to go a very long way."

"As far as murder?"

"Quite possibly." Lacey shook his head. "But why? He's calculating and would not kill somebody without a reason, and I can't see one with regard to Martha Shaw. Did they even know each other, Helen?"

"They certainly weren't friends if that's what you mean," she replied. "But he's been working regularly in Martha and Ruth's garden for some weeks now and he hangs around with the whole crowd of them in the Steamer. They've sort of adopted him because he's different. Like they are in another sort of way."

She turned to Maltravers. "Remember that argument I told you they had in there last winter? Nick was with them that night."

"Was he involved in the row?"

Helen frowned as she thought back. "Not as far as I recall. They were all sitting in that alcove by the window and he was stuck in the middle. When they all got going they just ignored him."

"And that was over Martha becoming a Roman Catholic," Maltravers recalled. "Can you remember any details of what they said?"

"No. Nobody took much notice until they really began going for each other and by that time they were bawling their heads off and it was impossible to make any sense of it."

"So we have a link between Charlton and Martha," Maltravers said.

"Yes, but I never saw them alone together and the village grapevine would have picked up anything like that," Helen argued. "He knew them all, but none any better than the others."

"However, he was working at the cottage when Martha was killed," Lacey added quietly.

"How do you know that?" Helen demanded.

"Somebody mentioned it to me when I got back to Porthennis this morning. I can't remember who."

Ice in Maltravers's gin clinked against the side of the glass as he rotated it in his fingers while he thought. Lacey was watching him, apparently waiting for him to speak.

"All right. He was on the spot, which means he could have had the opportunity," he said finally, looking from Helen to Lacey. "But you can't see any reason for him killing Martha."

"No, but what was he doing skulking around the cottage tonight?" Helen asked.

"There must be things worth stealing," Maltravers pointed out. "Perhaps nothing of great value, but enough to make it worthwhile. Have you any reason to think he's done that sort of thing in the past?"

"Not as far as I know," Helen replied. "I wouldn't trust him, but nobody's ever suggested he's actually criminal."

Maltravers glanced at Lacey. "Are your antennae picking up any vibes?"

Lacey shook his head. "I don't know what may be in Nick Charlton's mind, but I can't imagine he's taken to burglary by chance. There are plenty of other empty cottages in Porthennis if that was his idea."

"So is there something special in Martha's cottage?" Maltravers asked rhetorically. "And why does Charlton want to get his hands on it?"

"I don't know, but I can tell you this much," Lacey said. "And Helen knows this as well. Nick Charlton is much too calculating to take a risk — and after all Tess might have caught him — unless it was important."

"Like the evidence that someone murdered Martha?" Maltravers drew on his cigarette as he thought. "But that would mean he must have a reason to think she was murdered. You appear to be the only one saying that, Mortimer, and I can't imagine you've made the suggestion to him."

"I only talk to Nick out of unavoidable necessity," Lacey replied. "If he knows anything about Martha's death, he didn't hear it from me."

Maltravers leaned back in his chair. "So where do we go from here? Stick bits of bamboo under his toenails until he confesses?"

"It's awfully tempting, but I think I'll pass on that." Lacey returned Maltravers's look piercingly. "Try following your instincts, Gus. What do you want to do?"

"I think . . . What *do* I think?" Maltravers put his head back and gazed at the ceiling for several moments. "Nothing immediately occurs regarding this Charlton character, but without the slightest logical explanation, I think I'd like to see where Agnes Thorpe disappeared."

Helen stared at him in disbelief. "What on earth for?"

"Because ever since you told me about her in the Steamer, it keeps coming back," he replied. "Mortimer's telling me to follow my instincts and that's where they're leading me. Perhaps he can explain."

Lacey shook his head. "No, I can't. But if that is really what you want to do, you'd better get on with it."

Carved into the side of the land falling steeply from the moors to the sea, Fern Hill climbed straight up out of Porthennis until the whole village was visible behind Maltravers and Tess as they reached the level again. It was a Sunday-calm morning with few people about and the temperature was rising steadily. On one side of the road open fields ran upwards, on the other the land fell abruptly to immense wave-smoothed boulders piled along the beach. After less than a mile, they reached a five-barred gate, blackened with age and askew on rotting hinges, which took them on to a narrow coastal footpath squeezed between gorse and high ferns. Maltravers consulted Helen's Ordnance Survey map, annotated with neat pencil instructions.

"That must be Cat's Head." He pointed to where a rock with the necessary resemblance to those with imagination was fringed by the lace of low breaking waves. "We go down the next coombe."

An opening appeared in the brambles and gorse on their left as they walked on. Winding snake-like, the descent was shallow and the coombe was not overgrown. It appeared to be used regularly, although the tiny cove was empty when they reached it and climbed over the rocks to where the edges of the sea curled into thin scallops as it lapped the shore. Tess kicked off her sandals and walked out until water touched denim shorts then pulled off her T-shirt and turned to where Maltravers was sitting. "Catch!" She hurled the shirt to him, then threw herself forwards and began a slow, elegant crawl. He watched her swim almost to Cat's Head then turn and wave before continuing in an arc around the little bay.

"You're wet," he remarked as she waded back through the shallows, shaking long hair stained dark with seawater. "And this is not a topless beach. You have to appear at Penzance magistrates court in the morning, preferably exactly as you are."

Tess scattered droplets over him with waving hands before lying on her back on the warmed flat rock, hair spread out in a fan of shining rust, and closed her eyes.

"I'll teach you to swim one day if it kills me," she murmured.

"It's more likely to kill me," he replied. "I am living proof that the human body does not float in water, whatever science says."

He gazed round the cove, secluded and private under drooping greenery overhanging a cowl of land spooned out by the sea. The silence was broken only by the far-off purr of a speedboat, crumpled white ribbon of foam glittering in its wake.

"There are worse places to die," he remarked. "Wrapped in a shroud of peaceful water on a summer evening."

"Very poetic." Tess did not open her eyes. "Is that what happened?"

"That's the story." Ripples broke the surface of a sun-bright rock pool at his feet as he flicked a pebble into it. A disturbed crab scuttled along a patch of sand at the bottom and vanished under waving fronds of weed. "Agnes Thorpe came down here on her own and swam away to Avalon. Perhaps the last thing she saw was her theatre. Did you go out far enough to see it?"

"Just. You can see Cat's Head from the stage." Tess looked up at him, eyes crinkled against the sun. "Now we're here, have you any idea why you wanted to come?"

"Frankly, no," Maltravers acknowledged. "Why her body never turned up is a mystery everyone's forgotten now."

He twisted round and looked back up to where the outline of the coombe was just visible descending through the undergrowth. "But think of this. She leaves her clothes — or at least *some* clothes — here, possibly on this very rock, goes back to the path and walks to Morsylla — which is where we're heading — where somebody is waiting for her? Then the suicide note turns up and everyone assumes she drowned. It's plausible, and it explains why they never found her body."

"But why?"

"God and Agnes knows . . . Have you learned anything about her at the Botallack?"

"I've read about her in the permanent exhibition they've got," Tess replied. "There are photographs of what it was like when she started and the work in progress and a few details about Agnes herself."

She sat up, a half-moon of damp left by her hair steaming off the rock. Already the front of her body was almost dry.

"She was born in 1912 and her parents were fringe members of the Bloomsbury Group. She wanted to be an actress like her mother, but wasn't good enough. She had the idea for a theatre when she came here in the 1930s and started work on it when her parents died in a car crash three years later. Apparently they left her quite well off."

"A lady of independent means," Maltravers remarked.

"Yes, but not filthy rich," Tess corrected. "And she was careful with her money. Most of the Botallack was built by volunteers — including the original members of the Porthennis School — after the war."

"Helen told me that. It was what Agnes had begun that brought them down here," Maltravers said. "Did she ever marry?"

"No, but she was planning to."

"Who? One of the School?"

"No. Someone called Robert Jenkins who owned a pottery in the Midlands," Tess replied. "He was a widower and they met when he came here on holiday. Later he put money into the Botallack."

"A Black Country manufacturer with a soul?" Maltravers raised his eyebrows. "Or he must have been in love."

"It certainly seems so. After they officially gave up looking for her body, Jenkins still spent a fortune trying to find it . . . which knocks any idea she ran off with him on the head."

"What would have been the point anyway?" Maltravers agreed. "Perhaps there was someone else, but I'm only playing guessing games."

He picked up Tess's T-shirt and passed it to her. "Make yourself decent. You don't want to start a riot in Morsylla."

It was a spectacular walk above restless sea, the path now twisting down between centuries-old hedgerows of tangled hawthorn, elderberry, ivy and ferns, then climbing up again over crude steps hacked into the earth. It plunged through a belt of dark and cool conifers, dead pine needles packed beneath their feet, before taking them out into the open again and on to the highest part of the cliffs where they had to cling to clumps of coarse grass and edges of boulders as they stretched their legs across sheer drops that fell to liquid jade water noisily swirling in pits and crevasses. Eventually Morsylla appeared half a mile ahead, car-park and beach cafe at the end of a deep slash in the hills, their path now falling between white bells of convolvulus, beds of gorse and huge thistles. By a stone bridge over a stream, Maltravers took a photograph of Tess standing next to a towering gunnera plant which looked like the biggest rhubarb in the world, then they bought sandwiches and drinks from the cafe. As they sat on the boulders of the beach, he took out Helen's map again and pointed to Seal Bay, just over the next headland.

"We can reach the main road from there if we want and go back that way."

"I'd love to see seals," Tess said. "If you watch them, perhaps you'll learn to swim."

"Sure," he replied cynically. "And if they watch me, perhaps they'll learn to write."

Chapter Six

Swept in swift strokes, charcoal conjured perspective as Edith Hallam-West skilfully sketched the northern headland of Seal Bay, one of Cornwall's multitudinous tentacles groping the fringes of the Atlantic. Subtle smudges with her finger gave monochrome depth and distance to the horseshoe curve of cliffs and restless water beneath cloud-patched sky. In the foreground, firm lines shaped jumbled rocks and patches of sedge. She sat on a folding metal stool at the top of the beach, a slender figure in an emerald green trouser suit and broad-brimmed white hat. Maltravers and Tess saw her as they reached the crest above the bay and she looked up when their feet dislodged scatters of stones as they made their way down, then returned to her work.

"Good afternoon," Maltravers said as they reached her. He regularly defied English reticence over greeting strangers on a country walk.

Blue-green eyes looked at him above half-moon gold spectacle frames. She was seventy-three, the remains of what must once have been a very beautiful woman preserved in her face. Creases of age added a patina to ivory skin, enhancing without dimming, and still-abundant silver hair shone beneath the edges of the hat.

"Good afternoon. Gorgeous day." The voice was firm and educated.

"Glorious." Maltravers indicated her drawing. "May we see?"

"By all means." She held the paper at arm's length, examining it with casual criticism before turning the pad towards them. "It's only a working sketch though."

"As I can only draw breath and wages, I envy your talent," Maltravers said. "What will it end up as?"

"An oil." Her charcoal indicated a rock dominating the picture. "With a seal on there."

Tess looked round excitedly. "Are there really seals? Where?"

Edith Hallam-West laughed. "You're in for a disappointment, I'm afraid. They don't hang around sunning themselves when people come this close."

Tess turned to Maltravers in mock annoyance. "You promised me seals. I'm going to sulk."

"Perhaps this lady will paint one for you." Maltravers paused uncertainly. "Are you by any chance a wildlife artist called Edith something? I can't remember the surname."

"Hallam-West. How nice to be recognised. I'm flattered."

"I was guessing, but we're staying in Porthennis with Helen Finch and she's told me about the resident artists' School and at least part of your name stuck."

"Helen? Oh, yes." Realisation crossed Edith Hallam-West's face. "She mentioned you were coming. You're her cousin or something aren't you? The writer. I saw *Green In Judgement* on television. It was very good."

"Nice to be recognised. I'm flattered." They both laughed. "This is my girlfriend Tess Davy. She's appearing at the Botallack."

"Of course!" Edith Hallam-West stood up and offered her hand. "I was there the other evening and should have recognised you, although you look different off stage. I'll be coming again next week."

She smiled nostalgically, still holding Tess's hand. "I was taken to the opening night of *Private Lives* for my fifteenth birthday. The Phoenix Theatre, September twenty-fourth, 1930. Noël Coward, Gertrude Lawrence, Laurence Olivier and Adrianne Allen. It was my first visit to a real theatre — pantomimes didn't count — and I wore a grown-up dress of blue satin. I met the man who became my husband that night."

"I'm not sure I can match Gertrude Lawrence," Tess warned her.

"Having seen you play Shakespeare, I'm sure you'll make a good fist of it. I look forward to seeing how you do."

"Thank you." Tess frowned as she noticed gathered sadness pass across the elderly woman's eyes as their hands slipped apart. "And you met your future husband that night?"

"Yes. He was the son of friends of my parents and was in our party. Not that anything happened. Our eyes didn't meet or anything amazing like that. It only began three years later when we met again at Cambridge. We married straight after graduation." Abruptly she turned and looked across the bay. "We spent our honeymoon on the Black Sea. So long ago now."

Maltravers and Tess exchanged glances. Her appearance in one particular play had spontaneously triggered a lot of memories, and they did not all appear to be happy ones.

"What happened to your husband?" Maltravers asked.

"He was killed in the blitz in 1942." Catapulted into the past, Edith Hallam-West was speaking almost automatically. "Our son and daughter died with him. He'd taken them out for the evening and they were caught in an air raid. They should have gone to the nearest shelter, but they weren't far from home and must have decided to reach me. They wouldn't let me see the bodies."

Laughter of a family on the beach floated up to them as she suddenly shook her head fiercely.

"How silly of me, but . . ." She turned to face them again, apologetic and embarrassed. "It was talking about *Private Lives* that did it. I expect it's been at the back of my mind ever since I saw it was on. I'm sorry, I'm not usually as maudlin as this."

"That's all right," Maltravers assured her. "If you want to talk about it, we're good listeners. We have testimonials."

"But you don't want to be bored by an old woman." Edith Hallam-West closed her drawing pad and picked up her chair. "Anyway, I've finished here and you probably want to walk on."

"Not particularly," said Maltravers. "We've walked from Porthennis and if the seals aren't going to put in an appearance we're going back on the main road. May we come with you?"

"Only as far as my car. I'm too old now for five-mile hikes. I can give you a lift if you like."

Maltravers carried her chair as they climbed from the beach

73

and followed a path through a farm to where a red Mini, which looked as if it had been driven at least twice round the world, stood in a layby. Edith Hallam-West put her chair in the boot and they accepted an offer to run them back to Porthennis; Maltravers wanted to take the opportunity of asking other questions.

"We were talking about Agnes Thorpe earlier," he said as the car coughed into life, juddering as Edith Hallam-West forced it into gear. "You must remember her." He twitched apprehensively as the Mini leapt forward.

"Very well. I was one of her unpaid helpers building the Botallack. We were all younger then of course." She finally moved into second gear. "It was damned hard work. The only one of us used to lugging lumps of rock around was Patrick Dawson."

"Where did he learn to do that?"

"He'd been a miner in Lancashire. He went down the pits after his father died in an accident sometime in the thirties. Didn't stick at it long, but it built his muscles up. After that he joined the Merchant Navy which kept him fit. Then he was a Commando in the war. Made the rest of us look right namby-pambies."

She turned round to talk to Tess in the back, casually indifferent to road safety; they were already travelling at more than sixty miles an hour on a country road. "You know that arch on the left of the stage? The one you make your first entrance through? That was a solid piece and Patrick raised it into place on his own before it was carved and —"

"There's a bend coming up," Maltravers put in hastily and the car swerved sharply back into line. For a few minutes he mentally went over the terms of his will and contemplated which God he might have to make his peace with. Edith Hallam-West was continuing her story of the building of the Botallack, but he found it difficult to concentrate on what she was saying. Finally he asked another question.

"Agnes Thorpe was planning to get married around the time she vanished, wasn't she?"

"When she drowned herself. Yes." A meandering sheep

74

escaped instant conversion to mutton by the thickness of its summer fleece. "Chap called Hopkins or Jenkins or something like that. I only met him once. Potter; not making it, selling it."

"And you're positive she did drown?" Maltravers's hand gripped the fascia of dashboard, controlling a desire to grab the wheel as the car hurtled towards a black and white arrowhead board indicating another sharp bend at the bottom of a hill. There was a blur of hedges as they screeched round it. He glanced back at Tess; her eyes were closed and he was certain she was silently praying.

"She was dying," Edith Hallam-West replied; Maltravers identified with her. "She had cancer."

Mercifully they had reached a stretch of main road where space made Edith Hallam-West's driving marginally less homicidal.

"Had she told you that?"

"No. None of us knew until the suicide note turned up. She'd kept it to herself."

"What about her fiancé? Had she told him?"

"He said she hadn't." Left indicator flashing, Edith Hallam-West knocked several years off the life expectation of a cyclist as she turned right. She was still in second gear and they were back on twisting country roads.

"But there's still a mystery about . . ." Maltravers clenched his teeth and forced the word out, "about her body. Why was it never found?"

He wished he had not asked as Edith Hallam-West took both hands off the wheel in a gesture of incomprehension; smothered by the racket of the engine, Tess muffled a whimper of panic.

"Washed out to sea? Freak tide? Treacherous place Mounts Bay." Hands took control again after what seemed at least an hour. "Could have become trapped in underwater rocks. Nobody knows what happened. Why are you so interested?"

"No particular reason, but . . ." Maltravers spotted the gate where they had started their walk along the coast path in the morning. "Could you drop us here? I want to take some photographs."

"Where's your camera?"

He tapped a small square bulge in his shirt pocket. "Miniature one. Japanese." Brakes engaged savagely and his seat belt saved him from a serious encounter with the windscreen.

"Thanks for the lift." He held the front passenger seat forward for Tess to climb gratefully out. "Hope to see you again before we leave."

"I'll see you next week, anyway," Edith Hallam-West told Tess. "At the Botallack. You may hear me crying, but don't let it put you off. Goodbye."

The car roared off down the hill; one brake light was not working. Maltravers reached into his pocket and took out his pack of cigarettes.

"Good job she didn't ask to see the camera," he remarked. "I wanted a last one of these before I died."

"If she was fifteen in 1930, she's more than seventy now," said Tess. "Do they know she's on the roads?"

"It's not a thing they'd forget. My entire life passed before my eyes several times and —"

"And you weren't in it," Tess interrupted. "Very old, darling."

"Sorry." Maltravers took her hand as they began to descend Fern Hill towards Porthennis. Even close to the sea it was burningly hot, mirages of shimmering air on the road ahead of them. "However, it's been an interesting day out."

"If you like risking instant death."

"More than that," he corrected. "We know several things we didn't before. Not much, but put together perhaps they start to add up to something."

"What are you talking about?"

"Cambridge. The Black Sea. A pottery manufacturer and a Lancashire miner. Think about it."

"After what I've just been through, riddles I don't need," Tess told him. "You'll have to explain."

"It's too vague yet. However Mortimer was quite right when he said things would happen that would give us ideas where to look, but . . ." He shook his head. "But I didn't expect to be looking in this direction."

Hand in hand, they walked on past Martha Shaw's cottage and the studio where she had died.

Edward Cunnningham found it interesting to guess what customers who came into his shop would buy. His prices put many people off, but he offered a range of pottery seconds and smaller items which meant few left empty handed. He was watching a couple he had instantly labelled as yuppies deciding between a vase and a fruit bowl — his personal bet was on them having both — when the telephone rang in the office. Leaving his assistant to watch for shoplifters, he went to answer it.

"Patrick. Has Ruth been to see you?"

"No. Why?"

"She's got a thing about Martha. Reckons it wasn't an accident. She thinks someone pushed it."

There was a silence, before Cunningham spoke again. "You mean she thinks one of us pushed it."

"She didn't come straight out and say that, but she must do."

"Well you can count me out. I didn't do it."

"Neither did I." The denial was absolute. "What about the others?"

"You're serious aren't you?" said Cunningham.

"Ruth's serious."

Cunningham sighed heavily. "Dorothy, Edith or Belvedere? It's not impossible. That rock would have fallen over if someone leaned on it. What's Ruth going to do?"

"I don't know. The police apparently think it was an accident. Perhaps she'll let it go."

"And perhaps she won't. What should we do?"

"Keep our heads down," said Dawson. "And hope it goes away."

"You mean you don't think it was an accident either?"

"I want it to be. I'm getting too old to deal with anything else."

"We're all getting too old."

"Anyway, you know what to expect if Ruth turns up," Dawson added. "Tell her she's barmy. I'll see you Wednesday. It's Agnes's anniversary."

"God, I'd forgotten," Cunningham sounded weary. "Why do we still bother? It was a bloody lifetime ago."

"Because it's one of the things that keeps us together," Dawson told him. "I'll pick you up and give you a lift up the hill. Edith took me last year and I nearly wet my pants. Keep the bloody faith."

Dawson rang off and Cunningham remained seated at his desk, littered with scribbled orders, invoices not sent out and bills waiting to be paid. Filmed with dust, a forgotten invitation to a regimental reunion caught his eye and he tore it up and threw it into an overflowing tin wastepaper basket. Lance Corporal Cunningham, Army clerk, Royal Corps of Signals, 1939 to 1945, had no wish to be reminded again that he had been unable to fight. He swung his right leg out of the knee space in the desk with unthinking acquired skill of years and stood up. Only his oldest friends knew it was artificial; and they were about the only ones who remembered that war.

He stepped back into the shop where the couple had started querying prices with his assistant.

"That's how much it costs," he interrupted. "It's on the label."

"We'll think about it." The girl put the bowl back on the shelf. "We'll call in again."

"Bastards," Cunningham muttered as they walked out.

Maltravers searched among the display of local history booklets inside the door of the harbour front newsagents until he found one called *The Porthennis School and its Art*. He was leafing through it as he and Tess walked back to Lifeboat Row.

"First published in 1959, so it's a bit out of date," he commented. "But it's got potted biographies of them all . . . That's reckless Edith, the undertaker's friend, thirty years ago."

He held an open page towards Tess; more than half was filled by a photograph of Edith Hallam-West with a painting of a cormorant.

"Why did she never marry again?" Tess took the booklet for a moment to examine the page more closely. "She was beautiful."

"You can still see that." Maltravers rapidly read the text below the picture, then quoted: "'Edith Hallam-West began sketching wildlife during holidays in the Soviet Union with her husband. After he and their children were tragically killed during the war, she moved to Porthennis in 1948 to develop her talents — she had never been trained — under the guidance of Frank Morgan. Today she is widely recognised as a leading artist in her field and has illustrated several books.'"

He flicked through another few pages, pausing occasionally to read again swiftly, then closed the booklet.

"A very good two quids' worth," he remarked. "Let's see if Helen can fill me in a bit more."

"Do you really think you might have an idea who killed Martha Shaw?" Tess asked as they reached Lifeboat Row. "Just from talking to Edith Hallam-West and that book?"

Maltravers held the gate open for her. "Frankly, no. But I think I can see something, which is interesting . . . and might be important. I'll have to think about it."

Nick Charlton went to see Ruth Harvey that evening. As he had guessed, Dorothy Lowe was with the others in the Steamer and Ruth was alone, weariness of grief staining her face as she opened the door. She had returned to Martha's cottage because at least it offered memories for company.

"Hello, Ruth. I brought you these."

Unsure and embarrassed, he held out the bunch of carnations like a child, but chocolate-brown eyes watched her carefully. Normal friendly gestures did not come easily to him. Ruth looked surprised.

"Oh! Oh, how kind of you, Nick." She had received flowers from Edith, but suspected they were no more than a token gesture, probably sent after consultation with the rest of the School. Dorothy had passed on the baldest message of sympathy from Belvedere Scott and Edward Cunningham had not even been in touch. Patrick Dawson's final "Sorry about Martha", had casually dismissed the terrible end of the most important thing in her life in three words. She smiled at Charlton with gratitude and opened the door wider.

"Come in."

Inside the cottage, his eyes flickered snake-like at walls lined with books, heads carved by Martha Shaw on shelves in an alcove, the comfortable clutter of furniture and possessions accumulated over a lifetime by two people in love who had shared everything. He watched Ruth Harvey's thin body, trying to assess what it had been like when she was young, crudely imagining her in bed with Martha. Sitting in a plump fireside chair, he looked comically small, feet dangling several inches above the floor. Ruth sat opposite, thin hands clasped on her lap.

"It's nice to see somebody," she said. "Nobody else has been yet."

"Well, they're busy aren't they? With all the tourists."

"Yes, I expect they are, but . . ." Ruth shook herself, dismissing bitter thoughts. "Sometimes it's best to be on your own."

"Well I won't leave you on your own," Charlton assured her. "There's still the garden to look after and there's things need doing around the cottage. I can help you with, you know . . ."

He looked away uncertainly, confused by what were to him unnatural actions of kindness. Ruth interpreted it as embarrassment over the limitations of his handicap.

"That's kind of you, Nick," she said. "And I'd be very grateful, but I'm afraid I can't afford to pay you much. Hardly anything at all to be quite honest. You see —"

"I don't want money," Charlton interrupted, then lowered his head and mumbled the rest of what he had to say. "Miss Shaw — Martha — and you have been good to me and . . . and I don't have many friends."

It was a line he had carefully planned, certain that it would bring a sympathetic response; it worked better than he had expected.

"Oh, Nick," Ruth suddenly sobbed. "Martha was the only friend I had. I feel so dreadfully alone."

Charlton kept his eyes fixed on the carpet; she was not going to give him any problems.

Chapter Seven

"Whose yacht is that?"

"The Duke of Westminster's I expect. It always is."

Tess and Neil Levis paused as the laughter at one of Noël Coward's most famous exchanges went on too long. The audience should by now have adjusted to the surreal experience of watching the first act of *Private Lives* performed at the Botallack; two people on a hotel balcony overlooking an imaginary sea when the real thing was actually spread behind them. Tess waited until the laughter started to subside, then triggered a wave of hysterics with her next line.

"I wish I were on it."

Hysteria engulfed Elyot's reply that he wished she was on it too. Bewildered, Tess saw Maltravers sitting with Helen in the middle of the amphitheatre; he caught her eye and pointed behind her, shaking his head helplessly. It was impossible to continue and she filled the moment by casually turning round. Then she giggled.

"There's a bloody fishing boat out there!" she stage whispered at Levis. The audience spontaneously clapped as she turned back to face them, biting her bottom lip to prevent herself from losing control. Levis leaned his arms on the balcony rail and shook his lowered head.

"Does it pass this time every night?" he muttered.

"We're going to find out." Tess replied like a ventriloquist then returned to the script, relieved that there were no more maritime references.

"There's no need to be nasty."

Loaded down with its catch of plaice and turbot, the trawler

81

Cornish Maiden passed out of sight towards its home port of Newlyn, its skipper unaware of his inadvertent contribution to English comedy of manners. At the end of the play, Levis doubled the applause as he waved in acknowledgement at the shimmering backdrop behind them. Making their way out up the stone terraces with the rest of the audience, Maltravers and Helen met Edith Hallam-West with Dorothy Lowe.

"It was wonderful," Edith told him. "I did cry, but I laughed a lot as well. That fishing boat."

"Coward would have appreciated that," he said. "If you hang on, Tess should only be a few minutes."

"Good. I want to thank her. This is actually the first time I've seen *Private Lives* again. I don't think I mentioned that when we met the other day."

As the four of them neared the exit gate into the car-park, they passed Agnes Thorpe's statue, setting sun-cast shadow stretching behind it. The life-size figure held a book in stone hands, eyes eternally fixed on centre stage below. Maltravers stopped to read the inscription carved on the large square plinth on which it stood: "Agnes Matilda Thorpe, 1912–1951, founder of the Botallack Theatre. Lost at sea. Erected by her friends." In the bottom right hand corner he could just make out the initials MS.

"Did Martha Shaw carve that?" he asked. A few paces ahead, Dorothy glanced back at him.

"Yes. It's a very good likeness."

As the others walked on, Maltravers examined the statue's face. High cheekbones, long chin and 1940s-style rippling hair touching shoulders in waves of stone indicated intelligence and captured the streak of stubborn individuality she would have needed to build her theatre. The face reminded him of Edith Sitwell, but masculine, Plantagenet angles were softened by greater femininity. Sinking sun flushed the features with ghostly reality, amplifying Martha Shaw's skill in imitating life. He realised that Helen and the others had not stopped and followed them over the rise leading to the car-park.

"Would there have been a Porthennis School without Agnes?" he asked as he caught up with them.

Edith shrugged. "We might have got together somewhere else, but it all happened here because of her."

"But how did you all come?" he persisted. "Did you know each other before? During the war?"

"I met Belvedere after I ran away to France in 1932," Dorothy said.

"Ran away?"

"Oh, yes." She smiled. "I was quite the little Bohemian. My parents died in the First World War, father in the trenches and mother in the 1918 influenza epidemic the year after I was born. I was adopted by a wicked aunt and uncle straight out of a fairy-story. I took off when I was about fifteen and met Belvedere two years later."

"That was after he vanished, wasn't it? Helen's told me about him disappearing after his initial success."

"He'd got tired of the meaningless praise they poured on him," she replied. "He was very good — even brilliant — but he knew a great many people were only saying it because he had become fashionable. So he just walked away from it. He was living in a village in the French Pyrenees when we met, earning a living painting portraits for what local gentry there were."

"But when did you come to Porthennis?"

"After the war. We'd returned to England and London was depressing, so we came down here and offered to help Agnes. The School grew out of that. Frank Morgan arrived next — he and Belvedere had known each other years before — then . . . When did you come Edith?"

"The year after you, 1948. Remember I met you both on holiday?"

"Of course you did. My mind's going." Dorothy seemed annoyed with herself at forgetting. "Anyway, then Martha and Ruth moved in and Patrick brought Edward. They'd known each other in Spain. That was the lot of us . . . Oh, apart from Jonathan Bright, but we never really counted him, because he was such an appalling painter. In fairness he was the one who organised us though."

The last vehicles were crawling out of the car-park, noise fading as cinder dust thrown up from the surface settled again.

Tess waved as she appeared from the direction of the theatre in the twilight and Edith smiled and took hold of both her hands as she joined them.

"No, not Gertrude Lawrence," she said. "Nobody could be, of course. But you were awfully good."

"Thank you." Tess glanced out across the bay. "And at least we'll be ready for the interruption next time."

"You may not get it," Edith told her. "Newlyn fishing boats don't work to any timetables. They usually set off once they've collected the crew from the pub and return any time they've finished. They've operated like that since the Middle Ages and I don't imagine they're going to change their habits now. One might pass at the same time, but the odds are against it."

She smiled and touched Tess's hand again. "Anyway, we must be getting back. It was wonderful seeing you again and I hope you sell out for the whole week. You deserve to. Goodnight."

Maltravers appeared thoughtful as he watched the two women walk to where Edith had parked her car. It juddered into life then she drove off with a roar of acceleration reminiscent of Le Mans.

"If they've been going down to the sea in ships around here since the Middle Ages, they obviously know the tide movements backwards," he said to Helen. "Who's the best person to ask about where Agnes Thorpe's body should have been washed up?"

"Virtually any of the locals," she replied. "It doesn't even have to be a fisherman. But what on earth do you keep going on about Agnes for? That was forty years ago."

Maltravers shook his head in irritation. "I just keep coming back to that lady, but I'm damned if I can explain it."

"You mean you were serious when you suggested she might not have drowned?" asked Tess. "Could she have run away?"

"On what facts we have, it's possible," he argued. "Her body never turned up and there are questions about who told her she had cancer. It could all have been a cover story."

"But what for?" Helen demanded. "She was engaged to be married. Why should she run away?"

"Bad attack of cold feet?" Maltravers suggested. "With all the wisdom of hindsight, it would have been better for all concerned if Fiona had suffered from that rather than marrying me."

"Gus, it doesn't make sense," Helen objected. "She would have known it would look suspicious when her body wasn't found."

"But if it was suspicious once, it's not any more," he replied. "Now it's just the Porthennis mystery. She could have got away with it."

"And done what?" Helen sounded impatient. "As far as I know, she left all her money behind. What did she live on? Where did she — ?"

"Money?" Maltravers interrupted. "How much?"

"I can't remember exactly, but several thousand pounds. Quite a lot in the 1950s."

"And what happened to it?"

"After she was presumed dead, her solicitors carried out the instructions in her will. Part of it went to finishing the Botallack with the rest left to the Porthennis School. They spent most of it building an art gallery, but that was a disaster. They had to sell it in the sixties and it's a teashop now. So if she ran off, she had nothing."

"Not necessarily," Maltravers corrected. "How does anyone know that was all she had? If they'd discovered she had transferred *all* her money before her death, that would have been suspicious. But if she'd put part of it to one side . . . Come on, it's possible."

Helen turned to Tess. "How do you live with him? His imagination's worse than ever."

"He wasn't a writer when you knew him," Tess told her. "But he does make occasional guest appearances in the real world."

"When you've quite finished being a monstrous regiment of two women, perhaps you'd like to produce some *proof* that I couldn't be right," Maltravers said. "It is possible — all right, no more than that — but possible that Agnes Thorpe didn't die."

"And if she didn't, where does it get you?" Helen demanded. "What's it got to do with Martha's death?"

"There would have to have been a reason for her running away," he said. "Apart from her fiancé, the people she was closest to were the Porthennis School artists. Mortimer's convinced me that one of them could now have been murdered. There could be a connection."

"After all this time?" Helen protested. "That's insane."

"This thing's insane wherever you take a core sample. When dealing with the Porthennis School, it's best to put your rationality on hold."

"But if . . ." Tess paused, trying to adjust her mind to Maltravers's thinking. "But if you're right, then Agnes Thorpe could still be alive and . . . Are you saying she could have come back?"

"All suggestions gratefully received," Maltravers said cheerfully. "In this guessing game, it's impossible to be too outrageous. Yes, Agnes Thorpe could have come back, quite unrecognisable, perhaps just another old lady on holiday."

"And murdered Martha?" Helen shook her head. "That's ridiculous."

"Any more ridiculous than it could have been Belvedere? Or Dorothy? Or Edith? Or one of the others?"

"People that old committing murder?"

"I'm not aware there's an upper age limit on the activity."

Tess had turned to look towards Agnes Thorpe's statue. "But what is it . . . What could still be so urgent at the end of people's lives, that it would drive them to kill?"

"God knows," said Maltravers. "Perhaps some don't grow old, grey, full of sleep and resigned. Perhaps they keep the anger of being young."

"But I'm not thirty yet and what was important to me ten years ago doesn't matter now." Tess shook her head. "Gus, you've got to be wrong. It's out of all proportion."

"It's impossible," Helen added. "Things like that don't happen in real life."

"Real life?" Maltravers took Tess's hand as they walked towards his car. "Never underestimate what that can throw up.

You've both travelled around this country a bit. Have you ever come across a village, however obscure, which doesn't have a war memorial?"

"A war memorial?" Helen frowned at him. "I've never thought about it, but I don't think I have. What are you getting at?"

"I know of one in Gloucestershire," he said. "Men, and presumably women, went from it to fight in both world wars, but they all came back alive. When you see the crosses in the tiniest hamlets with the names of their dead, you realise just how incredible that is. Even Porthennis has one by the harbour, and a place as small as that lost thirty-six men in the First World War alone."

"And?" prompted Helen as he paused. "What's your point?"

"The village I'm talking about is called Upper Slaughter." Maltravers looked at both of them. "There's real life for you, and that's pretty damned impossible as well, isn't it?"

The dead leave little hauntings in the homes they shared with those they loved. Wandering aimlessly from room to room, Ruth Harvey found Martha Shaw everywhere. An old stain of spilled red wine on a carpet; a library book borrowed and never returned; a chipped Staffordshire pottery figure bought at a jumble sale; a blackened cigarette burn on the edge of a table; the sticking kitchen drawer which she had grumbled about for years. Every corner of the cottage bore echoes of her voice, reminders of her presence, touches of her personality; the very walls seemed to hold the living woman within their stones.

Ruth sat on a padded window-seat, evening light filling the alcove, and sadly turned the pages of a photograph album, snapshots dated in fading ink recording half a century. The earliest black and white pictures, taken on a box Brownie, were of vibrant young people; Belvedere Scott, the bearded golden giant, posing amid the chaos of building the Botallack; Edith Hallam-West, slim elegance unsullied by crumpled corduroy trousers and torn shirt; Dorothy Lowe with only the first suggestions of excess weight to come, sitting triumphant on the shoulders of Patrick Dawson and Edward Cunningham; Agnes

Thorpe caught in a rare moment when her quiet smile had bubbled into open laughter. And Martha, eyes filled with secret messages that only Ruth could read. As the photographs became coloured, the people in them imperceptibly inched into age. Hair went grey and thinned, bodies thickened, flesh fell slack, life drew patterns across faces, personalities matured out of the roots of youth. The last picture showed Martha in the garden, sitting on the faded canvas of a deckchair beneath pink cherry blossoms, metal frames of reading glasses catching the spring sun of three months before. Ruth stared at it for a long time, then gently laid her fingers on its surface like a pilgrim touching the relic of a saint, seeking some impossible, ameliorating sense of recaptured physical contact.

She put the album on the tapestry cover of the seat and looked through the diamond lead lighting of the window at Martha's studio, twenty yards away across flower beds and lawns. Who had slipped through that door while she had been preparing the evening meal at the back of the cottage? Martha must have known them, because she had continued with her work. Ruth's growing conviction that the death had not been accidental had not been voiced to the police because exposure of the murderer could reveal a motive she shuddered away from. But she had to know who it had been. Then she would decide what to do, how to expiate grief and anger as vivid in a woman of seventy-one as in tempestuous passions that only the young thought they felt.

While Helen was making coffee back at the cottage, Maltravers stood by the bookcase screwed to one wall, idly glancing through her collection of art books. One name on a spine caught his eye and he pulled the volume from the shelf and began flicking through the pages, stopping occasionally to look at coloured plates, mainly of Suffolk countryside. The paintings were skilful but not remarkable.

"I presume this is the Porthennis Frank Morgan," he said as Helen came through from the kitchen.

"Yes. Look at the section starting on page a hundred and two." She handed Tess her cup. "They're his masterpieces."

She watched as Maltravers reached the place, then slowly turned ten pages, eyes hardening with horror, then filling with pity.

"My God," he said softly. "Eat your heart out, Goya. Where can I see the originals of these?"

"Tel Aviv," Helen replied. "He gave them all to Israel when the state was formed in 1948. He refused to make a penny out of them."

"Which camp was it?"

"Belsen. He was among the first troops to enter it. He painted them later from memory."

Maltravers handed the book to Tess. "I don't think I could live with memories like that."

"The paintings helped him exorcise them," Helen said. "But nearly all his later work had some darkness in it."

Tess looked at no more than three paintings before closing the book with a shudder. "I can't stand that just before I go to bed. They're incredible, but they're too horrible."

Maltravers had gone to stand in front of the uncurtained window, looking out across the sleeping village.

"And when you've seen things like that, is Porthennis where you come to try and forget?" he asked reflectively. "Somewhere as far away as possible?"

"Frank Morgan didn't forget," Helen corrected. "Every year he made a pilgrimage to Israel. He didn't tell them he was the artist. He just spent hours standing in front of his own paintings again."

Maltravers's dreams that night were tormented by Morgan's terrible images of bestial inhumanity which dissolved into an awareness that he was in the Steamer watching a grinning dwarf who insanely changed into a baboon. Then he was irrationally standing on a deserted beach as the sea grew higher and higher and he was powerless to move. As the water relentlessly covered his face, he suddenly knew that he was dreaming and deliberately closed his eyes so that he could sleep within sleep and escape. He awoke sweating.

Chapter Eight

Tragedy struck the Porthennis School in 1951 when Agnes Thorpe, founder of the Botallack Theatre, which staged its first performances the following summer, was drowned. On the evening of July 18, she went for her customary swim at Cat's Head cove and did not return. Subsequently it was learned that she had been suffering from an incurable cancer and an inquest decided that she had taken her own life. Despite every effort, her body was never found.

Other members of the School erected a statue in her memory, the figure carved by Martha Shaw, and each year on the anniversary of her death, they visit the spot from where she disappeared as an act of homage to the woman who brought them together. There was an additional personal tragedy in that her death occurred only a few weeks before she was due to be married. The reputation of the Botallack is a permanent testimony to her dedication and . . .

Maltravers impatiently turned the page as *The Porthennis School and its Art* embarked upon another apotheosis of praise. The author had a sycophantic tendency to write about the School as though, comparatively, the Renaissance, Impressionists or pre-Raphaelites were no more than a bunch of enthusiastic amateurs who could paint a bit. But from almost reverent obeisance, occasional facts emerged, adding to the random pile in his mind which he would eventually have to try and sort out.

"It's the sixteenth today, isn't it?" he asked without looking up.

Tess remained behind the morning paper. "Yes, but don't worry. I'll remind you when it's our anniversary."

"Our anniversary is the twenty-ninth," he replied, lowering

the booklet. "We met at a dinner party in Chelsea when Harriet Meredith paired me off with an advertising agency copywriter called Jessica Beaumont. We were meant to have literature in common. You were stuck with Daniel Carlyle, a BBC television director who'd had a charisma by-pass operation. Jessica later had an affair with Harriet's husband, and Danny boy came out of the closet like an Olympic sprinter on steroids. Harriet is not one of nature's matchmakers. You wore a green Planet dress and had a stinking cold and fell madly in love with me when I produced endless Kleenex. The following week I invited you to —"

"All right, you've made your point," Tess interrupted. "Why are you suddenly interested in the date?"

"Because in a couple of days our neighbourhood geriatric arts colony is going to creak its way down to the beach for the umpteenth time in memory of Agnes. I'm thinking of being a fly on the wall, or at least behind a rock."

"Why? And how?"

"Because they may talk." Maltravers stood up as he replied and went into the kitchen and examined a local tide chart Helen had pinned to a minute cork board. "As to how, it's high tide at six thirty, so they won't be able to go right down on to the beach, even assuming they'd all be able to scramble over those rocks."

He returned to his chair. "Which means they will presumably stop near the bottom of the coombe where the ferns are thick enough to hide a regiment, let alone me."

Tess stared at him. "You're serious, aren't you?"

"Of course I am," he said. "Their emotions will be exposed. Agnes may be an old memory, but Martha Shaw's death is very close to them. I can't see them just standing there and saying nothing about it."

"But what do you expect them to say?"

"God knows." He shrugged. "Perhaps they'll just get nostalgic and sentimental. Some of them may even cry, although I wouldn't bet on it. But they'll be on their own and may say things to each other they would never say when anybody else is around."

"Is it really possible that one of them killed Martha?" Tess shook her head in continuing disbelief. "Even if they did, would they confess it to the others?"

"I don't know," Maltravers admitted. "But Mortimer's convinced me that Martha was murdered and I'm cast in the Sam Spade role. The obvious place to look is among the people who knew her best."

"Are you certain they'll be there?"

"Helen says they've never missed it yet and they're all still fit enough to make it."

"Well, they all seem to be faintly mad so you hiding in the bushes seems suitably bizarre. Don't sneeze."

As Tess returned her attention to the paper, Maltravers stretched out long legs and body, staring at the patch of bright blue sky visible through the open top half of the front door, and began to examine the ragbag of what he knew. Most of it was probably irrelevant, the difficulty was deciding which pieces had to be held to the light in a certain way so that they revealed something unexpected. He felt like an archaeologist trying to reassemble a collection of broken fragments without knowing what their original shape had been. But, however broken and distorted by time, there must once have been a shape. While his instincts kept sending him off in pursuit of the shadowy figure of Agnes Thorpe, common sense told him to concentrate on those who were certainly still alive. He stood up.

"I'm going for a walk."

"Well I can't come. I'm expecting that phone call this morning. Where are you going?"

"Edward Cunningham's studio and souvenir shop first. He's one of the School I haven't met so far. Then I'm going for lunch at the Steamer where I should find Belvedere. He's part of the fixtures and fittings."

"What do you expect to find out?"

"Possibly nothing." Maltravers flipped open a pack of cigarettes to make sure there were enough in it. "But they're not going to come to me, so I've got to make the running."

Tess took hold of his hand as he leaned down to kiss her. "Just be careful. Mortimer warned you this would be dangerous."

"I should be safe enough with a couple of pensioners just about old enough to be my grandfather," he said. "If they turn nasty, I'll kick their walking frames away."

"Don't joke. You still think one of them could have killed Martha."

"Which you think is mad."

"Yes. But it's more mad if it happened. And that sort of madness is frightening, darling."

"Don't worry," he assured her. "What can happen? Cunningham braining me with one of his pots? Belvedere clubbing me with his stick? I'm just a visitor having an innocent chat with them."

"But you could be treading on dangerous ground."

Maltravers pulled her long hair gently as he walked to the front door. "If I'm not back by nightfall, organise search parties." A shout of "Idiot!" followed him down the path.

The harbour front was experiencing one of its regular traffic snarl-ups as a minibus negotiated the sharp left turn to leave Porthennis, inching backwards and forwards as the driver swung his vehicle through the gap with the straining delicacy of a limbo dancer working at minimum altitude. Maltravers picked his way between a queue of cars waiting for the manoeuvre to be completed, then walked past the Steamer to where the road wound between houses to the other side of the harbour. Porthennis Potteries was in the corner of a small cobbled courtyard which it shared with a teashop and a diminutive Post Office and souvenir shop. There were only two people inside and they left a few minutes after Maltravers walked in. Conscious that the elderly man behind the counter was watching him, Maltravers spent several minutes examining some vases before picking up the most expensive.

"This is a limited edition I see," he said.

"That's right. Twenty-five only."

"It's beautiful."

Casually he carried the vase to the window to examine it in better light. It was shaped with the grace of a shell, translucent white, the glaze shining like a mirror, roses pale as though seen through mist skilfully baked into its surface. Could a man who crafted such a thing also be a murderer?

"There're cheaper ones if you want."

"No. I think I'll have this. It's magnificent." As Maltravers turned, he saw the look of satisfaction his decision caused. "I assume you made it? Edward Cunningham? I'm staying with Helen Finch and she's told me about you."

"I know Helen. Good painter." Cunningham took the vase and began to wrap it in tissue paper. His mood had changed from indifference at just another customer looking around to proper attention for one who spent good money. "You're a friend of hers?"

"Distant relation." Maltravers took out his chequebook. "Seventy-five pounds wasn't it? Payable to?"

"Porthennis Potteries."

Maltravers began to write. "I bought a book on the Porthennis School the other day. You were one of the founders weren't you?"

Cunningham's eyes flickered disparagingly as he placed the vase in a carrier bag. "That's ancient history now."

"But there are still several of you alive." Maltravers tore out the cheque and handed it across the counter with his bank card. "Most of the founder members as far as I can make out."

"We're down to six. It was seven until the other day."

"Pardon?" Maltravers affected momentary puzzlement. "Of course Martha Shaw. I heard about that, but I don't know the full story."

Cunningham was copying the number from his card on to the back of his cheque. He did not look up as he spoke again. "Piece of rock she was working on fell on her." He straightened up and handed the card back. "Accident."

"That's what the police say is it?" Maltravers pushed the card back into his wallet. "I assume they were called?"

"That's what they say. What else could it have been?" The hands holding the bag hesitated, almost as though the wrong answer would mean the vase would not be released.

"Nothing I can think of," Maltravers replied equably. "Same thing nearly happened to a friend of mine in London once."

94

"There you are then. Accidents happen."

Maltravers wondered if other of Cunningham's customers had raised the subject of Martha Shaw's death. The brief conversation had contained the suggestion of prepared responses to questions, like a government spokesman voicing the official line on something; an official line which was not to be questioned.

"They do indeed," he agreed, and was rewarded by the release of the vase. "Would you mind holding on to it for me? I don't fancy carrying it round the rest of the morning. I'll pick it up later."

"It'll be safe here." Cunningham accepted the bag back and placed it under the counter. "If I'm not in just see my assistant."

Maltravers left the shop clarifying his impressions of Edward Cunningham. Originally bantamweight body now carrying the settled ballast of what had started as middle-age spread; just enough hair remaining to defy baldness; a crease of faded scar tissue across one cheek giving what would otherwise have been an unremarkable face a highlight of drama. Another durable specimen of the old school, mentally alert, well preserved and able to produce pottery of real quality; the purchase of the vase had been a means of lowering barriers, but had also been well worth the money. And had there been overtones in his reaction to even an oblique suggestion about Martha Shaw's death? There had certainly been a sense of defensiveness, even defiance at any possible alternative to an accident.

As he strolled past cars parked on the harbour wall, until he was looking down at seawater washing softly through its entrance, Maltravers pondered the ramifications of his murder theory. A group of artists — eccentric perhaps, but not known to be actually lunatic — growing old together in a Cornish fishing village, then one of them suddenly killing another of the tribe? It was obviously implausible, but where else was there to look for suspects?

A little girl and her mother walked up behind him to join a man fishing, the little girl attacking a pink cloud of candy floss as big as her head. Watching the angler's rod flick weight and bait through a long arc into the water, Maltravers's sense of

95

disproportion deepened. People came to Porthennis for innocent pleasures, not dark and inexplicable passions; artists sold postcards and prints, they didn't murder each other; old people could be infuriating, but were harmless, even lovable if you were lucky. What could drive someone nearing the end of their life to kill a woman they had known for nearly fifty years? Lacey had talked of evil . . . Maltravers felt a prickle of apprehension, wishing he could conceive other motives, outrageous but less malevolent. Across the harbour, the windows of the Steamer glinted in the sun and he suddenly felt in need of a drink as well as talking to Belvedere Scott.

Slouched against the bar, the oldest of the old frowned uncertainly as Maltravers joined him, then made the connection with Helen.

"Hot again," he grunted. However unorthodox, he still instinctively responded to the British habit of comment on the current day's weather.

"And getting hotter," Maltravers replied as Jack Bocastle approached from behind the bar. "What'll you have?"

"Same again." Scott emptied his glass and pushed it across the counter and the landlord automatically refilled it from the rum bottle inverted into its optic measure. Maltravers ordered a pint of bitter and for a while let the conversation wander at Scott's pace and direction. With no audience to play to, the artist was in low gear, a performer relaxing between acts. Gradually, Maltravers edged the talk towards Martha Shaw, but Scott was uninterested. It had just been another death in a long life, unexpectedly precipitated, but it would have happened eventually anyway. It almost seemed to have been forgotten. Then Maltravers mentioned Agnes Thorpe and noticed a flinty wariness glitter momentarily in the rheumy eyes.

"It's always tragic when a body is never found. It seems incomplete somehow."

Maltravers made the comment casually, deflecting any suspicion that he could be especially interested by ordering more drinks for them both. Scott said nothing until the refilled glass was back in his hands, as though he had been weighing the remark and deciding how to respond.

"You're still dead, body or no body," he muttered sourly. "It doesn't matter. We're not all going to rise from the grave at the last trump."

"But there must have been a period when you all clung to the hope that she might still be alive," Maltravers added. "She could have been washed up exhausted somewhere."

"Well she wasn't." Scott nodded towards the sea, visible beyond the harbour through the pub window. "She's out there somewhere. What's left of her. She got her theatre, which was all that mattered to her."

"Are you really sure of that? That she's out there?" Maltravers decided he had nothing to lose by a frontal assault. "It seems to me that without a body, it could mean she never even went in the sea that night."

Scott's slouched, decrepit body visibly tensed. "What the hell are you on about?"

"She could have run away for some reason. Perhaps there was something she wanted to get away from. I know she was supposed to have had cancer, but Helen says they never found the doctor who —"

"She drowned!" Scott amplified the blunt assertion by slamming the base of his glass on the bar. "She'd got nothing to run away from."

"Well, you'd know of course," Maltravers replied, defusing Scott's sudden animation with respectful agreement. "You and the rest of the Porthennis School must have known her better than anyone."

"Ay," Scott agreed. "We knew her."

The third rum was swallowed and Maltravers wondered how much it would cost him to get Scott drunk and if it would be worth the expense anyway; the possibility of indiscretion might only dissolve into the reality of alcoholic confusion; and was there anything to be indiscreet about? He was whistling in the dark and possibly becoming confused by echoes. There were no concrete facts; however much Mortimer Lacey conjured up curious powers of knowing, there was only his unprovable insistence that Martha had been murdered as a starting point and Agnes Thorpe's disappearance had vanished into some twilight of legend. And were the two connected, apart from the fact that both women had belonged to the Porthennis School? He could see nowhere to go, but having made contact with Scott, decided to pursue matters and hope that something might possibly emerge.

"I've been reading about you in the booklet on the School," he said. "Is there any chance of seeing some of your work? Do you sell it?"

Scott snorted. "Yes, if you like third rate crap."

"No I don't," Maltravers told him. "But you weren't always third rate were you? Have you kept any of your old work?"

"There's a few still up at the cottage." Scott sounded dismissive. "But they're not for sale."

"And not even for looking at?" Maltravers let the question hang in the air for a few moments as the artist remained silent, then added, "I really would like to see how good you were once."

"What the hell for?"

Maltravers shrugged. "Because . . . no, it doesn't matter. They're your paintings, nobody else's. If you want to keep them to yourself, that's your business."

The rum appeared to be starting to have an effect, even on a system almost pickled in it.

"Yes, they're my paintings." It was as though he was speaking to himself and there was a reflective sadness in the words totally out of character with the abrasive, impossible old man. Maltravers caught Jack Bocastle's eye and another drink was poured. Scott stared into the contents of the glass for a long time before picking it up.

"Perhaps," he said.

Maltravers ignored the implied invitation and began talking about Helen, Tess, himself, anything but the Porthennis School. He bought Scott lunch and more rum, letting him lapse into his adopted role of mendacious raconteur and lovable local character. When they left the Steamer together, Scott was amiably lost in his own make-believe world and insisting that they both return to his cottage.

*

"There's absolutely damn all." Doughty gave his boss the information before he had finished reading. "We've looked everywhere and there's no motive. Nobody wanted to kill Martha Shaw."

Emsley ignored the remark and read on, then tapped a paragraph on one of the sheets of reports. "There's still this row in the pub that Jack Bocastle told you about."

"They're always bloody rowing," Doughty protested. "You know what old people can be like and that Porthennis lot have it in spades. Most of the time they just do it to amuse the tourists. Anyway, they were half pissed."

"What does Mike Nicholls think? He's the local beat copper."

"That it was irrelevant," Doughty replied. "He remembers one night a couple of years back when he had to tell them to pipe down when they were shouting their heads off about Martha Shaw making some sculpture for the head office of a London bank. Next day they're all pals again."

Emsley turned the page and read on for a moment. "And could that rock have fallen on its own?"

"Not on its own perhaps," Doughty corrected. "But if she'd been bashing away at it, anything could have happened. Those ladders of hers are lethal. Fall over as soon as you look at them."

"But it still could have been pushed." Emsley looked up sharply. "Couldn't it?"

"Yes, but who by?"

"Who was around? Ruth Harvey for starters."

"No way." Doughty sounded totally incredulous. "They were in love with each other. Had been for years."

"But we're not buying that without examining the goods," Emsley told him. "Lovers fall out and lovers kill. We know that well enough."

"Everybody says they were still devoted to each other," Doughty argued. "Ruth Harvey worshipped Martha Shaw — and we know she hardly benefited from her death. There's no motive there at all."

There were indications of agreement in the humming sound Ensley made in the back of his throat.

"And both a bit past it for someone else to have come in on the scene," he acknowledged. "All right, she looks highly unlikely . . . What about this character Charlton who was working in the garden. Bit shady isn't he?"

"Yes, but that's as far as it goes," Doughty replied. "He's never stepped out of line to our knowledge. Criminal Records say he's clean as a whistle."

"Doesn't look it," Emsley observed drily.

"We can't pull him in for questioning just because of the way he looks. They'd have us for dwarfism."

Emsley grinned. "Yes, tricky one that. But he was there."

"And there was nothing unusual in it," Doughty pointed out. "He'd been doing the garden regularly for some time, and they weren't the only ones in Porthennis he did it for. Let's face it, he's got to take what work he can. When you get down to it, the poor bugger's crippled."

"Let's not get over sympathetic," Emsley said. "If that rock could have fallen over as easily as you say, then he could have given it a shove as well as anybody. Do we know how strong he is? Dwarfs can be stronger than you think."

"What there is of him is thickset enough," Doughty acknowledged. "Not that it would have needed much strength. The thing was balanced on a knife edge. But why should it have been him?"

"He isn't going to tell us, so what can we come up with?"

"Sod all," Doughty said bluntly. "Nicholls has kept an unofficial eye on him for years — all right, he looks like a villain — but has never even got a drunk and disorderly on him. He's lived in Porthennis for more than ten years and is almost part of the scenery."

"Popular?"

Doughty shrugged. "Not what you'd call unpopular. Most people feel sorry for him. Admire him for hacking out a life without having to expose himself as a freak. He's a damned good gardener as well."

"Nice law-abiding occupation," Emsley remarked. "How did he and Martha Shaw get on?"

"According to Ruth Harvey, fine. Martha was a bit of a

gardener as well, but welcomed him taking the heavy work off her. A couple of days before she died they'd been discussing some changes he'd suggested."

"Discussing?" Emsley spoke sharply. "Not arguing?"

"Discussing," Doughty repeated firmly. "And she apparently agreed with them. He didn't kill her because she didn't like what he wanted to do with the herbaceous borders. I'm sorry, sir, but you're grasping at straws on this one. There's nothing to get hold of."

The inspector turned a page and read again for a moment. "Scene of Crime say they've identified more than thirty different sets of shoe prints on the floor of that studio. Did she hold parties?"

"It was open house," Doughty explained. "Friends, neighbours, tourists, anyone who showed an interest in her work. It hadn't been swept for months. God alone knows how old some of those prints are or how we'd trace who made them. And is there any point in trying when we can't see a motive and everything says it was an accident?"

Emsley looked at the file again, statements, medical and forensic reports, objective facts encapsulating what the police had pieced together regarding the sudden and savage death of Martha Shaw. It was his job to be suspicious, probing the most apparently innocent situation to see if there was a hidden and unexpected patch of corruption in it, to accept nothing at face value. But as more inquiries drew blanks, the original suppositions came back into focus, increasingly persuasive after surviving the pressure of examination. Untainted by contrary evidence, innocent and straightforward explanations were strengthened. It was happening with the death of Martha Shaw.

Nobody appeared to have a motive for killing her, nobody gained by her death, nobody had been threatened by her. The only notable recent thing in her life was that she had embraced Roman Catholicism, but she had done so quietly. She had not taken on the mantle of the bigoted convert, crying damnation on those who did not share her new beliefs. A statement from her parish priest said she had shown a marked sincerity, an anxiety to reshape her attitudes even in her final years, but it had been a private and personal anxiety. Religious conversion had led to a quarrel with her old friends, but apparently just the once. And there was nothing else, no suspicious strangers, no letters or papers indicating something wrong or inexplicable, no unusual patterns of behaviour. The facts suggested that Martha Shaw's death had been the result of a self-inflicted accident and the police had virtually run out of avenues that might lead elsewhere. Emsley handed the file back to Doughty.

"Pass it on to the coroner's officer," he said. "Unless something unexpected turns up, I can't see that the verdict's going to surprise anybody."

Chapter Nine

"Nick! Hello! I'm back. Where are you?"

Charlton twitched as Ruth Harvey called from the kitchen at the rear of the cottage; he had thought her visit to see Martha Shaw's solicitor in Penzance would have taken longer, leaving him more time to search. He instantly realised it was no use scuttling through the front door to pretend he had been working out there; Ruth would have seen him as she walked from the gate.

"In the front room," he called, his mind racing for a reason as he heard her approach.

"Nick?" She looked puzzled as she saw him. "What are you doing in here?"

"I heard the telephone." He gestured towards the instrument on a table near the window. "I came in to answer it."

"Who was it?"

"It was . . ." Deliberately he dropped one of his gardening gloves, thinking rapidly as he bent down to pick it up. "It was a wrong number. Somebody asking for . . . for Steve or someone."

"Oh." Ruth appeared satisfied. "Were there any other calls?"

"If there were, I didn't hear it ring. I only heard this one because I was working out the front." He moved towards her, away from the roll-top desk he had only just closed. "How did you get on with the lawyer?"

"All right." Ruth sighed. "There are just so many things to worry about. Have you made yourself a cup of tea?"

"Not yet."

"Well I need one. I'll bring yours out to you."

Charlton followed her back into the kitchen then went outside, remembering to go round to the front of the cottage where he began to tug weeds from dry, crumbling earth. He had been inside for more than an hour, starting in the bedroom and working his way through the rest of the cottage, looking everywhere for something that would give him if not an explanation, at least some clue. There had to be a paper, perhaps a diary, something, anything, that would reveal the truth he had glimpsed in the Steamer that winter's night. He had been cautiously sifting through the compartments of the desk and was just starting on the drawers as Ruth had returned. He had found personal letters to Ruth, receipts, the usual accumulation of leaflets from financial advice companies and magazine publishers mixed with flimsy glossy gift brochures, kept with the vague intention of looking at them sometime. But there had been nothing connected with Martha Shaw that gave him any information.

Upstairs, he had rifled a cardboard concertina file of papers that all seemed to relate to Martha Shaw. He had found correspondence about her work, more personal letters, invoices for a regular supply of herbal medicines. He had even flicked through a Bible on the bedside table, assuming it must have been hers and thinking something might be hidden inside, but there was nothing. Somewhere, he was convinced, there had to be an explanation of what lay behind the argument that had at first angered and then frightened the rest of the Porthennis School, possibly in the mind of the woman she had lived with, from whom she would have had no secrets?

"Here you are."

Absorbed in his thoughts, Charlton had not heard Ruth walk up behind him, carrying a mug with a sketch of St Michael's Mount stamped on it.

"Thanks," he said. "Just about finished here."

"The front wasn't that bad. Will you have time to tie up those beans before you go?"

"No problem."

Ruth smiled and turned away, her mind clearly on other things than the garden. Watching her disappear round the corner of the cottage, Charlton wondered what she knew, and how far he would have to go to get it out of her. There was too much at stake not to try anything.

In the kitchen, Ruth sat with her own mug clasped between thin hands. It had been a draining, emotional afternoon, the solicitor sympathetic, but inevitably reducing the greatest personal loss she had ever felt to questions of procedure and cold legal necessities. She had signed papers and agreed to actions in a growing daze, impatient with the ponderous stupidity of it all. Next there would be the horror of the inquest at which she would have to give evidence, the woman she had loved subjected to repulsive clinical examination and cold, official inquiries. Then Martha would have to be cremated and . . .

Ruth Harvey bowed her head and started to cry as the nightmare stretched endlessly ahead of her. But she would go through it for Martha's sake, carrying the unshakeable conviction that death had not found her by chance but had been deliberately precipitated. The determination to discover the truth of that put steely strength into the fragile little woman, enabling her to bear her grief, driving with an irresistible intensity.

Maltravers kicked aside a fallen fuchsia stem, peeled crimson bells of flowers limp and dying, as he accompanied Scott, mellow rather than paralytic, up the channel of stone steps that led to his cottage.

"Did that happen when you went down the other night?" he asked.

"Must have." Scott gasped the words out. "I went arse over tit just here." He rapped his stick on a stretch of flat dry earth between uneven stone rises up the side of the hill. "Grabbed at everything I could, but still ended up at the bottom."

Maltravers glanced back to where the steps fell thirty feet to the roadway below. Half-way down, a branch of a bullace tree, half snapped off, hung like a broken arm, splayed spikes of creamy interior wood ragged and darkening with exposure.

"Lucky you didn't break your neck," he remarked as they walked on.

"Only the good die young," Scott wheezed, then laughed sourly. "That's why we're all still going strong."

Marooned in a heaving green sea of overgrown garden, the cottage was as old, tired and crumbling as its owner. Pebbledash facing on the outside walls must have been white years before, but was now cracked and discoloured. Grubby dried-out paint was flaked and blistered on wooden window frames splitting with rot and the slate roof was fringed with drips of clinging moss. In the musty interior, patches of weave showed through faded worn carpets, wallpaper twenty years out of date was stained and peeling and the furniture would have disgraced a fire sale. But on the walls hung pictures that stopped Maltravers in his tracks.

The Palace of Westminster glowed beneath a Turneresque sky reflected in Thames water that almost visibly flowed; six women in a drawing-room captured mannered T S Eliot characters talking of Michelangelo; an afternoon in Hyde Park rivalled Seurat in its encapsulation of light; a portrait of a woman reading trembled with life. They were works of shining talent, produced by a man whose hands had been as skilful as his eye had been penetrating. Maltravers turned to where Scott was watching him, waiting for his reaction.

"So what happened?"

Even half drunk — perhaps because he was half drunk — Scott instantly absorbed everything behind the question. He scowled, looking at the paintings as though finding it difficult to associate himself with their creation.

"Success happened," he replied. "Sycophantic critics happened. Stupid women who wouldn't know the difference between a Bonnard and bloody brick wall happened. Men who bought art with as much feeling as they bought shares happened. I fucked most of the women, ripped off all of the men and pissed off out of it."

There was a residual sting of bile in the reply, a permanent licking flame of long-ago anger that had despised and rejected fashionable adulation and ingratiating flattery. Maltravers felt the surge of rekindled emotion and understood exactly why Scott had fled the role of society's idolised darling to live obscurely among illiterate French peasants who treated him as a man and an artist, not that year's cult figure. Did that capacity for rage still smoulder, ready to be reawakened by other catalysts, like an ageing tiger, teeth and claws retaining unsuspected strength to rip and destroy? And had Martha Shaw somehow ignited that dangerous fury? Helen had told him that Belvedere Scott did not even like himself. Coupled with such a fierce undercurrent of feelings transformed Scott from a scratchy eccentric into a rusty bomb, liable to explode if not handled delicately.

Obviously agitated by revealing an ancient, unsatiated resentment, Scott had opened a bottle of rum on the sideboard and poured another drink. He held the bottle towards Maltravers in silent invitation.

"No, thanks. Not after the beer."

Scott swallowed half the contents of his glass. "There's more in the other room."

Altogether, Maltravers counted thirty-three paintings, including two unexpected miniatures of wildflowers captured with fragile delicacy.

There was also a portrait of Dorothy Lowe, young, blonde, vivid and leaping out of its frame.

"Did you do any more of her?" he asked.

"A couple. The old bat's got them somewhere." Scott's eyes became puzzled and far away as he peered at the shining face.

"For you have forgotten that I loved you and I can't remember your name," Maltravers remarked quietly.

"What?" Scott asked absently.

"Just a line from a poem I never got around to finishing." Maltravers looked back at the portrait. "Is there any way you could get back there and do that sort of thing again?"

"No," Scott replied bluntly. "Edie's been going on at me about that for years, but that artist's dead. I killed him."

Maltravers felt an enormous surge of sympathy. The passing of love or the shattering of dreams hurt, but did not bite as deep as the permanent knowledge that a unique personal talent had been thrown away. Nothing healed that sense of loss. Whatever he had done — whatever he might even be guilty of —

Belvedere Scott was finally a man to be pitied. Suddenly uncomfortable with what he had stirred up, he glanced at his watch.

"I've got to be going. Thank you for letting me see your real paintings. They really should be exhibited."

"Not while I've got breath in my body." Scott dismissed powerful, confusing memories from his mind and Maltravers followed him into the hall. On a table by the front door stood a vase, its quality still shining through a filter of thick dust.

"Is that one of Edward Cunningham's?" he asked.

Scott glanced at it indifferently, as if reminding himself of its existence. "Yes. Ted gave me a pair as a birthday present when I was seventy-five. The other one's in my study. I keep brushes in it."

It was not quite the same as negligently using a Ming bowl as a chamber pot, but indicated Scott's cavalier treatment of a fellow artist's work. The lionised young painter of sixty years ago probably still retained a conceit of his own squandered abilities and looked down on the works of his friends.

As Maltravers stepped out into the sunshine again, he raised the real reason he had wanted to talk to Scott. The man was not going to suddenly slough off layers of abrasive hostility and expose his real self, but at least Maltravers had made some sort of contact.

"I've been thinking about Martha Shaw's death," he said casually. "It does seem to have been incredibly careless of her not to put some sort of support round that rock. Almost suicidal."

The mesh of lines running through Scott's face folded into different patterns as his eyes narrowed. However much he had drunk, there was still some compartment of his brain that could instantly register.

"What do you mean?"

Maltravers shrugged as he lit a cigarette. "I don't know, but if it was as precariously balanced as all that, it could have been pushed over very easily."

He had touched a nerve. For the briefest moment Belvedere Scott looked startled then a mask dropped into place.

"Balls," he said contemptuously. "Why would anybody want to do that?"

"No reason at all that I can see," Maltravers replied. "The thought just occurred to me."

"You bloody writers are all the same." Scott started to shut the door. "Too much imagination. Mattie died through her own stupid fault. Regards to Helen."

Just too quick, Belvedere, Maltravers reflected as the door closed. You should have either shown more interest or been appalled at the suggestion. The hasty brush-off was not the required response. Which means . . . God alone knows. He walked through the garden to the steps and made his way down, pausing to break off the untidy hanging branch and throw its remains into undergrowth vivid with the fire-orange of wild montbretia. In the roadway at the bottom was a dried, dark stain the size of a saucer. Maltravers stood by it, looking back up the steps to the spot from where Scott said he had fallen. Once again, the Almighty had looked after one of his drunks. And allowed a murderer to survive?

Maltravers started to walk away, when something that had not quite made sense clicked into focus. He turned and looked back up the steps. If Scott had fallen there, then surely he should have just collapsed in a drunken heap. But apparently he hadn't. Maltravers stood thinking for a few moments, trying to work out the ramifications of the suggestion.

"So did Humpty Dumpty fall or was he pushed?" he murmured to himself. "Pick the bones out of that."

Edith Hallam-West's lips pursed judgementally as she leafed through the sheaf of drawings, stopping occasionally to make the softest sound of approval, occasionally flicking over impatiently. Sitting by the long bay window of her studio, Helen watched her reactions carefully.

"Much better," Edith pronounced finally, picking up a handful she had placed to one side. "They're beginning to live, but the eyes are still giving you trouble aren't they?"

"Don't mention the eyes," Helen replied. "Cats have thoughts in them I can't understand let alone draw."

"All animals are the same," Edith said. "Now watch this."

For a few minutes, rubber and pencil erased and recreated. It would have taken a microscope to detect the eventual difference in the placing of lines, but suddenly life was captured in them.

"Edith, you make me want to give up," Helen said helplessly as she finished. "I just wasn't born with your talent."

"What we're born with doesn't matter. It's what we make of it." Edith tapped one of the drawings. "This is better than I could have done at your age. You'll make it."

Helen began to replace the sketches in her portfolio case. "Keep telling me that or I'll give up."

"Don't you dare, young lady." Edith smacked her wrist lightly. "There are no short cuts to being an artist. It's *work*. Look at this."

She led Helen to an easel bearing an almost finished painting of a kingfisher, brilliant with colour.

"This is the . . . sixth time, I think that I've tried to do it," Edith said. "Sometimes I've told myself that those colours only occur in nature and you can't find them in paint. But every time, I've got a bit nearer, and one day I'll make it. If I live long enough."

"You'll live to be a hundred. All of you will . . . oh, I'm sorry." Helen stopped and looked apologetic. "I'd forgotten about Martha."

"Don't apologise." Edith made what seemed an unnecessary adjustment to the position of the easel. "It was a great shock, but we're all coming to terms with it."

"Even Ruth? I really must go and see her."

"Then just remember she's very distressed," Edith said sharply. "Don't take too much notice of what she says."

"In what way?"

"Nothing particular. Just that . . ." Edith shook her head. "She seems to have some idea that it might not have been an accident. So silly."

Helen did not say anything for a moment, but thoughts rocketed through her mind. "What on earth does she mean, Edith?"

"That . . . No, it's just too ridiculous. I just felt I ought to warn you that she's being a little irrational at the moment. Just humour her. Now, you must excuse me, because I've got —"

"Edith," Helen interrupted firmly. "You can't just leave it like that. If Ruth thinks it wasn't an accident, what *does* she think?"

Edith Hallam-West sighed impatiently. "I shouldn't have mentioned it. She doesn't know what she's saying."

"But is she saying that she thinks someone pushed the statue over deliberately?"

"How do you know she's saying that?"

Helen frowned, startled at the force of the question. "I don't," she replied carefully. "But you said Ruth didn't think it was an accident, so what else was I to think?"

Edith turned away. "Yes. Well. I expect you're right. But, however upset Ruth is, it's inexcusable. Martha had no enemies. Who on earth could have wanted to kill her?"

"Nobody I know of." Helen decided to give Edith a way out. "But Ruth's emotional at the best of times and losing Martha must have upset her dreadfully. Don't worry. I'll try and calm her down."

She smiled and kissed Edith on the cheek. "Thanks for your help again. I'll keep doing it until I get it right as well."

Edith did not speak as Helen left the studio, then gave a moan of dismay as the door closed and she heard her footsteps walking away.

"Stupid, stupid, stupid!" she cried aloud as tears of tension erupted out of her. She crossed to the window and looked at the view without seeing the blurred blue horizon where the waves of Mounts Bay merged into the English Channel and distant Atlantic. The mention of Martha Shaw and Helen visiting Ruth Harvey had caught her off guard and she had revealed what Ruth was privately saying to plant the suggestion that it was ridiculous in Helen's mind. But she had done it all wrong; in trying to dismiss it, she had shown too much concern. Helen was too observant to have missed that, but surely she would not pursue it? Surely she would simply accept that Edith had been upset by Ruth's hysteria and its implications? Surely she would be understanding and sympathetic? Surely she would never suspect there had been anything more to it? Surely, she . . . ?

"Stop it," Edith told herself firmly as her imagination began to run riot. "It's all right. She can't know anything."

Chapter Ten

"You stupid, bloody thing!" The toe of Helen's soft canvas shoe made violent contact with the front of her automatic washing machine and she hopped in pain. "Ouch!"

Maltravers's head appeared enquiringly round the door of the minute wash-house on the other side of the narrow passageway behind the cottage. "Something wrong, dear heart?"

"Oh, you're back." Helen glared at the machine. "This damn thing's playing up again."

He looked down at stubbornly silent electric gadgetry. "A case of it toils not neither does it spin?"

"Very funny, but I'm not in the mood," Helen snapped crossly. "I'd ask you to look at it if you weren't so hopeless. You'd probably plunge the whole of Porthennis into a power cut."

"Don't underestimate me," he corrected. "Turn me loose with some instrument of advanced technology like a screwdriver and the entire West Country would be at risk. Why don't you revive ancient traditions? Take the clothes down to the river bank and beat them between two stones, singing the traditional chorus of the Cornish washerwoman."

"Thank you, but I'll use the launderette in Penzance." She groaned. "But the car's in for service. That's why I'm at home today. Giving me a chance to do the damned washing."

"I cannot bear to see a maiden in distress," Maltravers told her. "I'll run you into Penzance."

"Maiden?" Helen repeated cynically. "Come on. Even my memory's not that good. All right, thanks. Half this lot is yours and Tess's anyway. I'm looking forward to ironing a man's shirt again."

Maltravers looked reflective. "Didn't you once put a white one of mine in with a red blouse and it came out a rather fetching mottled pink?"

"I was very young at the time."

They bundled up the washing and, as they were leaving, Helen commented on the carrier bag Maltravers had left on the chaise-longue.

"It's a vase I bought from Edward Cunningham," he explained. "It's superb. I'll show you later. I've also been enjoying Belvedere's company . . . and perhaps something came out there."

"Oh, I've got something to tell you as well," Helen said. "I took some of my drawings up to Edith earlier. She's given me a lot of help in the past. By chance Martha's death came up and there was . . . I can't quite explain it, but it made me uneasy. It was as though she felt she had to convince me that Martha's death really was an accident."

Maltravers stopped by the gate. "Edith? But I got those sort of vibes out of Belvedere. We'd better exchange notes."

By the time Maltravers had parked in Penzance and they had reached the launderette, they had listened to each other's experiences and bounced ideas around until possible patterns had crossed the borders from bizarre to insane.

"The trouble is," Maltravers said as he helped load the clothes, "if Martha was murdered by another member of the School, the roots of it almost certainly go back a long way and how do we investigate it? There has to be more to it than that row in the Steamer about her becoming a Catholic. That sanitised booklet doesn't tell me anything and, as you've said, they all guard their secrets."

He shut the circular glass door and began to feed coins into the machine. "And from where I'm standing, Agnes Thorpe still won't go away. I know it doesn't make sense, but with Mortimer around who's looking for normal? Anyway, it's occurred to me that there could be other people in Porthennis, who aren't connected with the School but who were here when she vanished. If there are, I'd like to talk to them and see if anything comes up. Any suggestions?"

"The obvious one is George Trevithick," Helen said. "He's been retired for years, but he was the local bobby when Agnes vanished."

"Was he indeed?" Maltravers looked at her questioningly. "How's his memory?"

"Fine as far as I know. He was certainly still perfectly lucid when I saw him a few weeks ago."

"And the Agnes Thorpe case was probably the biggest thing in his career," Maltravers added thoughtfully. "I can't imagine that policing Porthennis and the neighbouring villages was as hectic as patrolling downtown Chicago. He's going to remember it."

"But what's he going to remember?" Helen asked.

"I don't know, but there's a permanent loose end with Agnes Thorpe. Her death was presumed, but never proved. It would be interesting to find out exactly what the police thought about that off the record."

"Gus, we've been through all this," Helen argued. "If Agnes Thorpe didn't drown —"

"Then what happened to her?" he interrupted. "Obviously we can only guess, but if you take that possibility, however remote it is, as your starting point, you've got a whole new ball game. If I could find a reason why Agnes might have wanted to get away from Porthennis — and convince people she was dead — then maybe a few more things would fall into place. She was part of the Porthennis School, in fact she began it. Mortimer's now convinced us that Martha Shaw was murdered and the most likely suspects all worked with Agnes. To our certain knowledge, two of them are getting twitchy. Chasing after Agnes may be a shot in the dark, but what else is there to go on?"

For a few moments, Helen watched the internal gyrations of the machine in front of them.

"All right, it doesn't make any sense, but I expect it's worth trying," she agreed finally. "And there's somewhere else you can look. Somebody wrote a book about Agnes. It was only published locally and I can't remember its title or the author, but the library should have a copy."

"Did it cover her disappearance?"

"As far as I know it did."

"Where's the library?"

Helen pointed down the street outside the launderette. "Morrab Road. About ten minutes walk that way. On your left."

"Don't let the washing burn. I'll be back shortly."

After he left, Helen picked up a magazine from the bench where she was sitting and idly read her horoscope. "This is a week when you will feel increasingly bewildered and uncertain. An old friend will return into your life and bring excitement, but beware the risk of hasty romance. There is unexpected news from a strange quarter and you will face difficult decisions which will affect the lives of others. Lucky colour blue, lucky day Tuesday, particularly the afternoon."

She was quite impressed until she looked at the magazine's cover; it was nearly six months old.

Hand on the raised lid, Ruth Harvey sat in front of the desk as the brass carriage clock on top of it struck seven slow, mellifluous notes. The instant she had seen the inside, she had known something was wrong. The desk had belonged to her parents and Martha had never used it; amid the casual, comfortable disarray of the cottage, its contents were the only things kept impeccably in order, a legacy of childhood conditioning carried for a lifetime. While it was not now untidy, things were fractionally out of place. The corner of a piece of paper protruded over the edge of a closed drawer, a tin lid containing postage stamps was not in front of its usual compartment, a half-used packet of envelopes had been pushed back into its slot so that the flap of one was bent.

As she looked, other tiny irregularities visible only to her began to appear. She tried to remember if she had opened the desk since Martha's death, distressed and indifferent to how she left it, but it was only now that she had decided she could face starting to write the inevitable letters. Then she remembered she had returned home to find Nick Charlton in the room. He had been standing . . . Where? Over there, by the telephone table under the window? No, much nearer the desk. And he had dropped something as he was talking. What had it been? A gardening glove. But once when she had offered him a pair, he had told her he never wore them, holding out strong, clumsy hands, resistant to scratches and dirt, mute evidence of years of manual work.

"Oh, no," she groaned. Nick Charlton had been trying to rob her, taking advantage of her grief and vulnerability. His offer to help had only been a way of deceiving her, of gaining access to the cottage to probe for valuables. What had he taken? There was nothing worth stealing in the desk, but . . . She hurried upstairs to her dressing table. Her mother's engagement ring, the diamond pin Martha had bought her in Hatton Garden, her dead brother's gold watch . . . all safe in the worn morocco jewel case in the drawer. And so was the money, nearly three hundred pounds in a roll of notes, withdrawn to pay a workman who wanted cash but still had not turned up to collect it. Anxiously, she tugged off the elastic band and counted them; none had been taken.

She closed the drawer, eyes taking a mental inventory of ornaments and valuables. Nothing appeared to be missing. She had been out that afternoon for more than two hours and Nick Charlton could have stolen anything he wanted. If it had not been for the evidence of the desk, she would not have thought about it, and weeks might have passed before she became aware that some familiar object had disappeared.

Slowly she went downstairs again, trying to understand. Was Nick just one of those people with an obsession to glimpse other people's lives? Had he been looking for — she grimaced with distaste — women's clothing? It made no sense, but she had no doubt that he had searched her desk, although there was no sign he had been anywhere else. What had he hoped to find? It was only after turning the riddle round every way she could, that the fact he had been working in the garden the day Martha had died came back to her. And she had been busy baking. Which meant she would not have noticed if he had gone into the studio and . . .

And deep down, the conviction that someone had murdered Martha had hardened into certainty.

"Interesting?" Helen asked. Maltravers did not reply as he flicked over another page and continued reading the biography of Agnes Thorpe, a mind honed against the deadlines of journalism rapidly absorbing essentials and discarding irrelevancies.

"Good writer," he murmured appreciatively. "Sticks to the facts."

He turned back several pages. "At first the police apparently considered the possibility that she'd not died, but went off the idea after the suicide note turned up. But that proves nothing. If she wanted to give the impression she'd killed herself, that's exactly what she would have done. Where does this ex-copper of yours live?"

"George? End of the terrace next to the Methodist chapel at the bottom of Fern Hill. You can't miss it. It's got a pair of painted sailing boats set in the pillars on either side of the front door."

"Can you come with me? If he knows I know you, he might be more agreeable."

"All right, but I still think you're wasting your time. Even if Agnes Thorpe didn't die, why on earth should she suddenly come back now and have some connection with Martha's death? Surely you're not suggesting she murdered her?"

"I'm not going that far," Maltravers assured her. "At least not yet. But is the idea that some other member of the School may have killed her any more outrageous?"

"No," Helen admitted cautiously, then shook her head. "But not Edith. She's a sweetie."

"Don't let that fool you. Underneath, Edith Hallam-West is as tough as old boots. They all are and . . ." Maltravers glanced through the open top half of the front door as he heard the latch click on the gate. "Ah, the very man. Mortimer, we need to pick your brains. Or your senses."

Lacey leaned his elbows on the bottom half of the door. "What have you found out?"

"Odds and ends which don't make much sense, but what would your instant reaction be if I mentioned Agnes Thorpe?"

"Agnes Thorpe?" Lacey savoured the name like a connoisseur assessing some rare vintage. "It's so long ago that it's buried too deep in people's minds for me to pick anything up about it. But I've never been completely satisfied that the whole story has ever come out."

"Gus thinks she might not have died," said Helen.

"I wouldn't . . . say that was impossible." Lacey opened the door and stepped into the cottage. "But that's just my feeling. Have you got anything more definite?"

"Frankly, no," Maltravers confessed. "I'm just collecting pieces of the jigsaw and wondering how — or if — they fit together. Not having the picture on the lid doesn't help."

"I'm sorry I can't help you by saying you're on the right track," Lacey told him. "But I can't say you're on the wrong one either."

"Very useful," Maltravers said drily. "Are you a Libran?"

"Yes."

"I thought so. So am I. The problem with Librans is that they'll always give you a definite maybe."

Lacey grinned. "Astrology? I wouldn't have thought you believed in that."

"I don't, but I contradict myself. I am large, I contain multitudes. Which is just as well, because I'm dealing with multitudes here."

"Six is a rather small multitude," Lacey commented. "You must have narrowed down your suspects to the Porthennis School."

"Yes, but I'm discounting Ruth," Maltravers replied. "The sixth has got to be Charlton, our miniature joker in the pack."

"But he certainly had no connection with Agnes Thorpe," Lacey pointed out. "I'm not certain how old Nick is, but I don't think he was even born when she disappeared, and by Porthennis standards he's still a newcomer to the place."

"True," Maltravers agreed, then stood up with a grunt of

frustration. "Seen through a glass darkly, this is all incredibly complicated, but I think it may be quite simple if I can just find the bloody key."

"Is murder simple?" asked Helen.

"At the bottom line, yes," Maltravers said. "Or at least the reasons behind it are. The motives of killers are positively pedestrian."

"Only if they're pedestrian killers," Lacey added quietly. "But not if they're mad."

"Mad?" Maltravers echoed. "You mean that?"

"Oh, yes." Lacey sniffed. "Can't you smell madness in the air round here?"

"No, and I don't think I want to."

"Well it's there."

Maltravers dropped his shoulders in mock despair. "Mortimer, you're as much comfort as an empty bottle to an alcoholic."

"I bring you naught for your comfort."

"Quotes I don't need," Maltravers told him. "Particularly any that go on about the sky growing darker and the sea rising higher. Anyway, Helen was just about to take me to see George Trevithick who may be able to come up with more details about Agnes's disappearance."

"Good thinking," Lacey said approvingly. "Give him my love . . . better make that best wishes. I don't want him getting any wrong ideas. Once a copper, always a copper."

George Trevithick was Cornish Peninsular Man. During their conversation, Maltravers realised that he had never travelled further east than Exeter, a rare excursion into another county, apart from one trip to London to receive an MBE for faithful policing of the tiny corner of England that had been his family's home since before the Domesday Book. A widower, he lived alone, but two of his sons were still within a few minutes' walk; the third had moved to some *terra incognita* called Welwyn Garden City, a place as remote and unknown to his father as Tibet. Age had rusted his joints with arthritis and stroked the drooping moustache with chalk. He had long memories, roots running miles deep, a circle of friends being slowly diminished by death, his television set and a ragged, amiable mongrel comfortably into his second canine century. Trevithick welcomed company, particularly any which gave him the opportunity to talk about the past.

"Agnes Thorpe?" he repeated after Helen had explained. Their cover story was that Maltravers was thinking about writing a newspaper article on the mystery. "Never did get to the bottom of that."

"But there was an inquest," Maltravers pointed out.

"Only because Superintendent Hawkins and Harry Tomkins, the old coroner, wanted to keep things tidy. Both dead now of course. When we couldn't find her body and that note turned up, they were satisfied."

"But were you?"

Trevithick pulled a face, then stood up and went to an oak dresser in one corner of the room. He opened a drawer and Maltravers could just see that it contained a collection of dark red notebooks, neatly arranged and obviously old. He took one out and glanced inside the cover.

"Here we are. Beat reports from January to October 1951. I've kept them all." He sat down again and turned several pages, then handed the book to Maltravers. "Read that. Everything I can tell you's in there."

Its foundations laid by a village schoolma'am, fading script swept across the lined pages in firm, classic loops, the letters leaning slightly forwards. George Trevithick had been a conscientious and meticulous policeman, noting everything that happened in his career in plain but comprehensive narrative. The account of Agnes Thorpe's disappearance covered twelve pages, each entry dated and frequently timed, until the final comment: "Inquest held at Penzance coroner's court, September 3, 1951. Verdict: suicide."

"You say . . ." Maltravers turned back several pages, "that after she hadn't been washed up along the coast here, the search moved to the far side of Mounts Bay. That's quite a distance isn't it?"

"Call it four miles in a straight line east to west," Trevithick replied. "But Agnes was a strong swimmer. She could have made that."

"Do you think she actually did?"

"I'm going no further than saying she *could* have done," he repeated. "But there were others who thought the same. Old Dolly Pentreath — long before your time, Helen — was convinced of it."

"Why?" asked Maltravers.

"Because she met Agnes on the afternoon of the day she vanished and swore that she was perfectly normal."

"She didn't seem upset about anything?"

"No." Trevithick paused and Maltravers sensed the old policeman's anticipation of revealing something with a little drama. "But she was coming out of her bank in Penzance. When we checked later, they told us she'd drawn out a hundred and fifty pounds in cash."

"Enough to run away with?" Maltravers suggested.

"You could live on that sort of money for a long time in those days. And we never found hide nor hair of it."

"But her death was still presumed and the inquest went ahead?"

Trevithick sniffed disparagingly. "A few people senior to me decided there was enough evidence for it. Particularly with that note."

"Can you remember what it said? Even roughly?"

Trevithick paused, then quoted without further hesitation. "'I have taken my life because I have contracted cancer and have only been given six months to live. The doctor has warned me that the end will be painful and I do not choose to face that or inflict the distress of it on those I love. It is my wish that they will continue the activities of the Botallack Theatre and the other plans we have made, as a permanent memorial to one who loved Cornwall.' Might have got the odd bit wrong, but that was it more or less. I've got a copy somewhere if you want to see it."

"No, your memory's good enough for me." Maltravers completed his final shorthand outlines, then read it back quickly. "Where was it found and who was it addressed to?"

"It came through the post to Dorothy Lowe the day after Agnes vanished. Posted in Penzance."

"Where she'd been seen that afternoon," Maltravers commented. "Why Dorothy Lowe?"

"Nobody knows, but she was secretary of the Botallack Theatre Trust, or whatever they called themselves in those days."

"I didn't know it came in the post," said Helen. "I thought it had just turned up at her home."

"Two other things," added Maltravers. "Did she write a letter to her fiancé and was there a will?"

"Jenkins said she didn't and was very cut up about it," Trevithick replied. "But her solicitor produced the will. Basically, everything was left to the trust. The others confirmed that all their wills said the same thing."

Maltravers frowned as he looked back over what he had written. "I take it the police were satisfied that the note was genuine?"

"In her handwriting and on her notepaper."

"And despite all that, you and others here in Porthennis still didn't believe it?"

Trevithick absently stroked the head of the half-asleep dog sitting by his chair. The animal's wagging tail slapped softly on the floor in the silence.

"We thought there could be another answer," he said finally. "But we didn't know what it might be and had nothing to prove anything. She was certainly never seen again, alive or dead."

He accepted a cigarette, leaning forward in his chair as Maltravers reached across and held out his lighter.

"George, if it had been up to you, what would you have done?"

The old policeman expelled a slow stream of smoke. "I'd have waited a damned sight longer before I held that inquest. In fact, the file could still be open on it today."

"But surely she would have died by now?"

"Possibly, but possibly not. She'd be getting on, but no more than a few others I could name in this village. Like me."

Chapter Eleven

Imperceptibly, the silent room slid into gloom, lemon evening light fading down through amber and monochrome twilight and dying in soft grey shadows. Ruth Harvey's mood darkened with it as the possible, chilling reason behind Nick Charlton searching the cottage began to obsess her. At first it had been inexplicable, but then she had begun to piece together random incidents and apparently casual remarks and an explanation began to emerge that first shocked then persuaded and horrified her. He had been so very clever, hiding his intentions behind a façade of helpfulness and sympathy, as he plotted, invidiously creeping towards the truth he had somehow glimpsed. Searching the cottage would not have helped him, unless there had been something hidden there that Martha had never told her about, which she could not believe. But what would he do next? There were other places, perhaps containing things Ruth did not know, other people who might be tricked into fatal indiscretions.

Suddenly she became conscious of the gathered darkness. She stood up and turned on the standard lamp by the window. The shade was reflected in the glass as she stared into the night at polished ebony sea. It was nearly half past ten, and the last light of the day had been smothered by a cover of cloud. She had to think what to do. Martha would have known, but Martha was now only a great hollow emptiness in her life, an emptiness caused by whoever had killed her. Had it been Nick? Or had it been . . . ? Her mind reeled with possibilities. If she could only talk to Martha. No, not talk, that was impossible, but communicate somehow. At the end Martha had believed there was life beyond death and perhaps . . . the image of Agnes Thorpe's statue formed in Ruth's mind. She shuddered but accepted its summons. A few minutes later, she drove up Fern Hill and took the road to the Botallack.

Before leaving George Trevithick, Maltravers had asked him to point out on a map where Agnes Thorpe's body should have been washed ashore. It was a quarter-mile stretch of coastline, starting on the opposite side of the Botallack headland from Cat's Head cove, jagged with tiny inlets too small to have even been named. Trevithick assured him that every one had been searched, but Maltravers set off early to collect Tess after the evening performance and walked along the edge of the cliffs to see for himself where it should have happened. Looking down at huge granite rocks stained saffron with lichen and washed with smoke-grey sea, he turned over what he had managed to discover, frustrated as they stubbornly refused to yield their secrets, if secrets they had. There were clear connections between Agnes Thorpe and Martha Shaw when both had been alive; now one was certainly dead and the other . . . ? A coroner's verdict could not kill her, nor an old policeman's suspicions make her live. And only Maltravers's own irrational instincts linked them both. Idly he kicked a stone and watched it tumble down before bouncing off the face of a rock and dropping into the water with a splash he could see but not hear.

An hour later, he was still as helpless as he removed the tape of Barbirolli conducting Elgar and replaced it with the Gerry Mulligan quartet. The tenor saxophone playing the 'Morning of Carnival' theme from *Black Orpheus* drifted across the empty Botallack car-park and into the whispering night as another car drove in and stopped near Agnes Thorpe's statue. Little more than a silhouette in the darkness, someone got out and he was peering across the distance between them, trying to make out what the figure was doing, when the passenger door opened and Tess joined him.

"What are you staring at?"

"Over there." He nodded in the direction without looking at

her as he turned off the music. "By the statue. Just standing there."

Tess squinted. "Who is it?"

"I don't know. They've only just arrived. Come on, I want to know what's going on."

Their footsteps crunched on a crisp foam of cinders, but Ruth Harvey remained motionless as they approached, head bowed and hands clasped, then jumped and looked startled as they reached her. Pallid moonlight gleamed between rags of tearing cloud and glistened on quicksilver streaks of tears.

"It's all right," Maltravers said gently. "We don't want to disturb you, but we just saw you here and wondered . . . Are you Ruth Harvey?"

"How do you know?" The question was guarded, even afraid.

"I didn't, but . . ." He glanced at the statue. "Martha carved that didn't she? Is that why you came?"

"Who are you?" Now the question was timid.

"We're friends of Helen Finch. I think you know her. I'm Augustus Maltravers and this is my girlfriend Tess Davy, who's playing here at the Botallack. I've just come to collect her." He hesitated. "We know what's happened of course, it must have been terrible for you. We're very sorry."

A sob choked in Ruth Harvey's throat before her voice emerged in a strained whisper. "Please . . . it's very kind of you, but please leave me alone. I'll be all right."

Tess looked at her sadly. "You must have loved her very much."

Ruth Harvey's eyes became empty, as though she was gazing inward at a lifetime of memories in a great sweep of recollection. Pressed tightly together, thin lips trembled.

"Yes," she replied and there was unutterable sense of loss in the single word. "She was everything I had."

Tess felt the swarm of Ruth Harvey's feelings reach them. It was as though the agony of every tragedy she had appeared in was concentrated on this elderly and vulnerable woman, helplessly crushing her.

"It will get better." Maltravers's assurance was totally inadequate, but he had to say something. Ruth Harvey turned to the statue again.

"No, it will never get better," she said softly. "Not until I am dead myself."

"Oh, you mustn't say that," Tess urged her. "You mustn't think it. Friends of mine have died, people I loved very dearly. It's awful and the pain never completely goes away, but it does become bearable."

"I'd like to believe that, but you see . . ." She shook her head violently. "No, there are things I can't talk about."

"Of course you can't," Maltravers said sympathetically. "We all have secret memories of people who were special to us."

"Secret memories." The phrase was repeated thoughtfully. "But not always happy secrets. Sometimes they're wicked."

Appalled by the word, Tess instantly interpreted it in only one way. "No! You mustn't say that! It wasn't wicked. You and Martha loved each other. I know people must have said it was wrong, that's how they thought when you were young. But it wasn't!"

"What?" For a moment Ruth Harvey appeared confused, then understood and contradicted her. "Of course that wasn't wicked. It can't be wicked to love someone."

"Then what do you mean?"

"I mean that . . ." The little woman stopped herself savagely. "No, I mustn't! Go away. Please."

"You mustn't what?" Maltravers pressed gently. "It's important isn't it? Perhaps we can help if you'll tell us."

"Help?" She looked at him in bewilderment. "Nobody can help. Not now. It's too late."

He stepped forward and took her arm as she began to sob. "Ruth, this is a dreadful question, but I have to ask it. Do you think that somebody killed Martha?"

She wrenched herself away, staring at him in terror.

"What do you know?" The cry of her question filled the night.

"I don't know anything, but . . ."

"Was it you?" Ruth Harvey backed away. "It was, wasn't it?"

"Of course it wasn't. I never even met Martha. I'd not heard of her until . . ."

She suddenly leapt at him, frail hands hysterically beating his chest. He wrapped his arms around her tightly.

"Stop it!" he said firmly. "It's all right. Nobody's going to hurt you. Come on."

She struggled helplessly, then her head fell against him and she began to cry, shuddering with emotion as he hugged her like a child. Tess put her hand on the old woman's trembling shoulder.

"We didn't hurt Martha," she said gently. "But do you know who did?"

They waited as wracking sobs slowly subsided into nervous shivering, then Maltravers felt her slacken in his grip.

"I'm sorry." The agonised croaking voice was desperate and pleading. "I'm being very stupid."

Maltravers let his arms fall as Ruth pulled herself together. She sniffed loudly and pressed the back of her hand against her nose.

"I'm just very upset and you saying what you did made me . . ." She looked up at him, eyes asking forgiveness. "You get silly ideas when you get old. Of course nobody killed Martha. Why on earth should they?"

"I'm very sorry I upset you," he replied carefully. "I'm the one who should be apologising."

"It doesn't matter." For a moment, her eyes went back to the statue. "I shouldn't have come here."

Abruptly she turned and walked towards her car. Tess made a movement as if to follow, but Maltravers caught her hand and silently shook his head as he led her away.

"She's terrified about something," he murmured. "If we press it in the state she's in, all we'll do is upset her even more."

He opened his own car door. "Get in. I'm going to stop along the lane and wait until she leaves. We'll follow her and make sure she gets home safely."

He pulled into a passing place within two hundred yards of the theatre and turned off engine and lights. It was very quiet. Far below, cloud-free moon turned patches of sea into hammered pewter as it splashed about the crouching black form of Cat's Head rock.

"You do realise that she could throw herself off the cliffs while we're waiting here, don't you?" Tess said.

"It's a risk." Maltravers blew cigarette smoke out of the

window. "But if she really is suicidal, she's going to do it anyway. Nobody can watch her night and day."

"What do you think? About what she said."

"She's lying. At least at the end she was covering up by pretending she was being hysterical. She believes Martha was murdered and must have different reasons than Mortimer for thinking it."

The cigarette end spun like a glow-worm in the darkness as he flicked it on to the road. "And what was it that was wicked? That's a heavy word for a little lady."

"She's very distressed," Tess said. "Don't pounce on everything she says and start analysing it. She just lost the woman she loved."

"Point taken, but Helen and I stumbled across a few other things today," he replied. "Any suggestion to other members of the School that Martha's death wasn't an accident touches very raw nerves."

Tess remained silent for a few moments after he had finished telling her about Scott and Edith's reactions.

"But you've really got no more than impressions," she said finally. "There's nothing positive."

"I know that," he acknowledged. "But the impression is that they know something and want to keep it covered up."

"And does Ruth know something as well?"

"She accused me of murdering Martha, which . . ." Maltravers thought for a moment. "Which suggests she may not actually *know*, but suspects. And where does she come tonight? To Agnes Thorpe."

"To a statue of Agnes Thorpe carved by Martha Shaw," Tess corrected. "That's not quite the same thing."

"But if she just wanted to be close to something Martha made, there are almost certainly things of hers in the cottage. Why come out here at this time of night?" Tess frowned disapprovingly, but said nothing as he lit another cigarette. "I've been looking into that little mystery again as well. Helen took me to see the old village bobby this afternoon and he's never really believed that Agnes died."

"Then what does he think happened?"

"He doesn't know, but even after all these years he's still not satisfied about it and . . ." Maltravers, who had been watching the rear view mirror, reached for the ignition key. "This looks like Ruth." Seconds later an old Ford Escort went past and Maltravers pulled out.

"Don't get too close," Tess warned him.

"Don't worry. I don't think she'll recognise us anyway."

As they reached the top of the Fern Hill road, they saw the Escort's brake lights flare as the car stopped. Maltravers killed his headlights and they watched Ruth Harvey go through the gate of the cottage. As they drove past, a light appeared behind the front room window.

"At least she's home safe again for the time being," Maltravers said as they cruised down the hill and into Porthennis.

"What are you going to do next?"

"Think." Maltravers hauled the steering wheel from right to left and right again as he negotiated the narrow street zig-zagging down to the harbour, houses pressing in on either side. "I've believed Mortimer right from the start and Ruth confirmed it tonight without meaning to. Martha Shaw was murdered, but there's not enough to go to the police with yet. Somewhere in this ragbag of bits and pieces we've picked up, there have to be some answers."

He braked as a cat scuttled in front of him and vanished into the shadows of an alleyway. He peered after it. "Was that black?"

"All cats are grey in the dark," Tess quoted. "But it could have been. That's lucky."

"Not everywhere," he corrected. "In America — and in some parts of Britain as well — it's bad luck. Wonder what they believe in Cornwall?"

Mortimer Lacey was having a late drink with Helen. When Maltravers and Tess had completed the story of meeting Ruth, he stared at the floor, tips of elegant fingers tapping lightly together.

"What do you think?" Maltravers asked. "Any idea why she was there?"

"No," Lacey replied. "Ruth's always been the quiet one and I haven't met her more than a handful of times. What I can't understand — and this is common sense, not mysticism — is if she thinks Martha was murdered, why hasn't she gone to the police?"

"Perhaps she doesn't know who did it," Helen pointed out.

"That doesn't matter," said Lacey. "If she thinks someone did it, she must also know why, or at least suspect something. All she has to do is reveal a possible motive and let the police take it from there. But as far as we know, she's going along with the accident theory. At least in public."

"Might it help if you met her again?" Maltravers suggested. "You might pick something up."

"Possibly," Lacey acknowledged. "But Ruth's obviously keeping a lot of things secret and I've already told you that I can't see everything hidden inside someone's head. If I could, I'd be making a fortune as an interrogation consultant with MI6. I'll try and casually run into her, but I'm not offering any guarantees."

He smiled at Maltravers. "I have many limitations. I'm afraid I can't produce answers like rabbits out of a hat."

"Pity," Maltravers commented. "We could do with a bit of magic."

"You're doing all right," Lacey assured him. "There's a lot bubbling to the surface at the moment and I think you'll sort it out eventually."

"Your faith touches me. Like the man said, we have a riddle wrapped in a mystery inside an enigma. But what is underneath all the layers?"

"A murder," said Lacey. "At least we're all certain of that now, aren't we?"

After Lacey had left and Helen and Tess had gone to bed, Maltravers sat at the dining table with his notebook. Apart from his conversation with Trevithick, he had written nothing down, but a short-term capacity for almost total recall — invaluable in his reporting career — enabled him to go back over everything that had happened and record it, remembered conversations and comments, fragmentary information and impressions. When he had finished, he sipped his gin and tonic as he read his notes back, then picked up *The Porthennis School and its Art* and read parts of it again. Hazily, vague connections began to suggest something, but would not coagulate. He went to bed, mind crowded by personalities of disturbing failed artists, passions and old secrets unknown and impenetrable.

Shortly after dawn, Tess half awoke as a seagull screeched on the roof. She rolled over, instinctively reaching for Maltravers, but the bed was empty. Drowsily she patted the sheet then blinked her eyes open before turning towards the low window beneath the sloping ceiling. The curtains were partly open and he was sitting in the tiny window seat looking towards the still and quiet morning harbour. Outside, the air was a shimmering veil of shining milk white and incredibly pale lemon. Light from the rising sun was made richer as it gleamed on orange curtains. For a few moments she watched him, but he seemed totally unaware she had woken up.

"What's your story, morning glory?"

"Mmm?" Absorbed in thought, he sounded surprised to find he was not alone. "Sorry, did I disturb you?"

"No, but that damned gull did. How long have you been awake?"

"About an hour."

He turned to the window again and Tess sat up, now looking at him in concern. "What's the matter?"

"I think I've come up with something," he replied. Caught by the tone of his voice, Tess waited, but he did not speak again.

"Hey, come on." She took hold of his hand encouragingly. "Tell momma."

Maltravers gave the faintest possible laugh and there was no humour in it. "I don't think momma's going to like it. I certainly don't."

"What is it?" His mood was beginning to worry her.

"All murders are unforgivable, but this one could be particularly nasty." For a few moments he watched scavenging gulls swoop and settle on the harbour sand, cries faint but clear in the morning silence. "You shouldn't kill someone just because you disagree with them."

"Is that what happened?"

"Let's just say it's a theory that grotesquely fits the facts. Now I'm going to have to try and prove it."

Chapter Twelve

Everything had to seem normal. Radio 4 voices filled the kitchen, even though their chatter and laughter was monstrously irrelevant. Ruth tackled the *Guardian* crossword as usual and the challenge of the clues at least occupied her mind as she forced herself to eat toast and lime marmalade. When Charlton arrived she wanted nothing to suggest that things were any different; he was more likely to be careless if he did not suspect anything. As she was finishing the second slice of toast, she heard footsteps outside and glanced at the clock. Why was he early? He should not be here for another . . .

"Only me." The back door opened and Dorothy Lowe stepped in, a wicker basket covered with a linen tea cloth hooked over one arm. Wearing a blue denim dress belted at the waist, she resembled a plump, elderly district nurse. "Anything left in that pot?"

"What?" Her mind conditioned to face Charlton, Ruth was confused for a moment. "Oh, yes . . . You know where the cups are."

Dorothy put the basket on the table and went to a wooden rack on the wall, taking down a mug.

"I've been cooking." She helped herself to milk and an alarming amount of sugar before picking up the teapot and starting to pour. "Had a bit of steak and kidney to spare, so I made you a pie. There's some scones in there as well. They'll keep in your freezer."

She sat down and rested her elbows on the table as she drank. "Know you're perfectly capable of looking after yourself, of course, but it's silly not to accept help at a time like this."

"Thank you."

For a few moments neither of them spoke again, but Dorothy watched Ruth's pinched face closely over the edge of the mug. She looked much older, like a fine Victorian china doll, glaze cracked and gone dull.

"How are you feeling?" she asked.

"I've not slept very well, but it could be worse."

"Should get something from the doctor."

"He gave me some pills. They help me sleep, but I have nightmares." Ruth took a handkerchief from the pocket of her flowered dress, holding it in readiness for the tears she could feel beginning to sting. "I keep seeing . . . you know. How I found her."

Dorothy reached across the table and took her hand. "I know. It must be dreadful. But at least she didn't suffer."

"The police told me it would have been instant." Ruth pulled her hand away and looked down uncertainly. "Dorothy, I know you think that I'm not as clever as the rest of you — I'm not — and that I can be silly —"

"Ruth, don't say that," she interrupted.

"No, it's true. It's always been like that. I only became part of the Porthennis School because of Martha." She smiled regretfully. "She never said it, but even she thought my poetry was dreadful and she was quite right. But you know how much we loved each other."

Dorothy took another mouthful of tea, eyes remaining fixed on the liquid in the mug as she lowered it again. "You're still one of us. You always will be. Nothing can change that."

"Look at me Dorothy." Ruth's voice was unexpectedly firm and her eyes had become piercing as the other woman faced her again. "Martha's dead and nothing can bring her back. But I have to know something."

"Know? Know what?"

"If somebody killed her." The statement was made perfectly naturally, its implicit "of course" unnecessary.

"Oh, Ruth!" Dorothy stood up. "Now stop this nonsense at once."

"But is it nonsense?"

"Of course it is. You know the police are satisfied it was an accident."

"But their saying it doesn't make it true does it?"

The radio was still on, and the silence after Ruth's question was ludicrously filled by a man talking about East Anglian dialects and superstitions.

"But it *is* true." Dorothy sounded over-patient and slightly patronising. "You're upset, Ruth. You're not thinking straight. It's quite understandable."

"I'm not as upset as I was," Ruth corrected. "And I think the reason is that I'm becoming angry."

Dorothy sat down and took her hand again, this time holding it so firmly that she could not let go. Her voice became insistent.

"Ruth, this is unforgivable. You know what you're saying, don't you? Martha's death was a terrible accident and nothing more. You must believe that."

"Yes I must, mustn't I?" she said bitterly. "Shut up, Ruth."

"I don't mean it that way! You must accept that it's true. Nobody killed her. Why should anyone want to?"

"Oh, Dorothy," Ruth sounded reproachful. "Let's not pretend you don't know that."

"Well I don't."

"Now I know you're lying," Ruth said simply. "What else are you lying about?"

"I'm not lying about anything! You're not well, Ruth. You're upset. You're . . ." Dorothy stopped as the little hand was jerked out of her own with sudden strength.

"Mad?" Ruth challenged. "Go on, you might as well say it. That's what you mean, isn't it?"

"No, but . . ." Dorothy gestured helplessly, "but irrational. You're imagining things. Just let it go."

"That's what you want me to do, isn't it?"

There was another silence, then Dorothy sharply pulled the cloth off the basket, took out the pie and plate of scones, and slammed them down on the table.

"I'm not going to waste my time trying to talk sense to you in this mood," she snapped. "Are you coming tonight? For the anniversary."

"Oh, yes." Cadences in Ruth's voice took the reply far beyond a simple confirmation. "I'll certainly be there."

Dorothy glared at her furiously, then turned, crossed the kitchen in three swift strides and pulled the back door open to leave. Charlton was standing on the step outside, raised hand clenched into a clumsy fist.

"Morning, Dorothy. I was just about to knock."

Appalled by what Maltravers was suggesting, Tess had wanted to discuss it with Helen and Mortimer, but he had told her to say nothing.

"It will only condition the way they approach it from now on," he had said. "They'll instinctively look for things to support it and might miss something that explodes it. And that's something I'd like to happen if possible."

As Helen was preparing to leave for work, he casually asked a question. "Do you still have that Chambers dictionary I bought you once?"

"Yes. Not one of the most romantic presents I received from a boyfriend."

"But probably the most useful," he commented. "Your spelling was atrocious. And at least you still have it, which is more than can be said for all the flowers and chocolates the others turned up with."

"It's in the bookcase in my bedroom. Bottom shelf I think. See you this evening."

As she left, Maltravers went upstairs then came down holding a thick red volume, pausing on the bottom step to read the inscription he had forgotten he had written inside the front cover. It was a simple code leading to a series of definitions which spelled out a very bawdy message.

"What are you grinning at?" Tess asked.

"Never mind. It's private." He flicked to the back of the dictionary and ran a finger down one of the columns. "Well, well, well. I never knew that."

"Never knew what?"

"See for yourself." Tess looked where he was pointing. "Only a little piece, but it fits the pattern doesn't it?"

"Yes, but it's a bit thin," Tess argued. "It doesn't *prove* anything."

"Proof, I'm afraid, may have to be at a premium. I may never get further than educated guesswork."

"And then what?"

"Then I may have to face somebody with it."

"Who?"

"If I knew that, I wouldn't be guessing."

"So how do you find out?"

"This evening could be . . . . illuminating."

"What's happening this evening?"

"The Agnes Thorpe memorial meeting."

Tess no longer needed to ask how the unexplained disappearance of Agnes Thorpe could be connected with the murder of Martha Shaw.

Long fingers of roots creaked as Charlton pulled at what was left of the wisteria; planted by the cottage wall years before, it went far and deep into the earth. Sinews and blood-choked veins strained on his forearms and stubby fingers gripped with the unbreakable strength of a bulldog. Slowly the soil began to give, then there was the sound of brutal tearing and stretched roots snapped and were wrenched out like a stubborn tooth. For a moment he stood gasping, sweat dripping from soaked eyebrows; there were not many men of any height who could have done it.

He wiped his forearm across his face, crumbs of soil mixing with dripping perspiration to form sticky smears of dirt. He needed a drink. It was surely time to be offered coffee, but he wanted something longer and colder. Perhaps Ruth had remembered to buy some beer. He walked from the front of the cottage towards the back kitchen door, outside which he had stopped and stood for those vital few minutes that morning when he had heard raised voices. Every unguarded word had been audible through the open window and every one had told him again that there was something unexplained and capable of frightening. Infuriatingly, not enough had been revealed, but if he had wanted further proof that he was on to something, now he had it. And now he knew something else. Ruth Harvey believed that Martha Shaw had not died accidentally; that had to be handled very carefully.

"Hello?" he called. "Ruth? Are you in?"

He waited on the step, the considerate gardener who did not want to tread dirt into the house. The kitchen was empty, but Ruth's open handbag was on the table and the radio was still playing. So she had not gone out, but could be upstairs. He called again, but there was still no response. Cautiously he went inside.

In the hall Ruth stood very still. It was such a clumsy little trap, but worth trying. Her ears strained, then she heard the faint rustle of paper. She closed her eyes, drew in a deep breath and stepped into the kitchen doorway, forcing herself to speak normally as she entered.

"I'm sorry, Nick, I was upstairs. Were you . . . ?"

He looked like a guilty schoolboy, grimy fingers still holding the paper he had taken out of the open envelope she had deliberately left there, an estimate from a plumber to repair the bathroom cistern. But he looked like a very nasty schoolboy.

"What are you doing?" she asked.

"Searching your handbag."

The admission was blunt and almost indifferent. Caught without any possible excuses, Charlton had instantly decided he had nothing to lose by the truth. His mask of helpfulness had been wiped away to reveal something repulsive and menacing.

"What are you looking for? Money?"

"No. I think we'd better have a talk."

Ruth dragged courage out of herself. "The only thing I have to say to you is get out of here at once. And please don't come back."

He ignored her, dropped the paper on the table and closed the back door. Then he climbed on to a chair and pointed to the one opposite.

"I'm not leaving. Sit down."

"No, I will not!" Ruth injected another burst of simulated anger into her voice to hide her fear. "If you don't —"

"Sit down you stupid cow or I'll break your fucking neck!"

He nodded slightly as she obeyed with a little whimper. "That's better. Don't worry, I'm not going to hurt you. Unless you give me no choice."

"What do you want?" False courage of seconds earlier had been instantly suffocated by Charlton's explosion of viciousness and the whispered question was consumed with dread.

"I want you to tell me things. About Martha and the rest of you."

"What do you mean? What things?"

"About what you were all on about in the Steamer. January it was. I was with you and Martha was going on about becoming a Catholic and then everyone started rowing, but I couldn't follow it."

Ruth Harvey suddenly understood a great deal. "I don't remember it. Was I there?"

"Of course you bloody were. Sitting with your orange juice. Didn't say anything, but you were there all right."

"Well I can't remember it. Why does it matter?"

"You remember well enough. And you know why it mattered."

"If it did matter, why is it so important to you?"

"That's my business."

Ruth picked up the estimate, folding it into its envelope before putting it back in her handbag. She had forgotten Charlton had been there on that horrible night when the others had been so awful to Martha. She had tried to defend her, but had been swept aside, ignored as usual. She had been relieved when Jack Bocastle had sternly told them that unless they stopped it he would throw them out. They had quietened down, but the resentment and anger had simmered on until she and Martha had left. It was an evening she had tried to forget, until Martha's death had brought its rage swarming back.

"Well?" Charlton demanded.

"I'm not going to tell you. It was nothing to do with you. I don't care if you hurt me."

Spoken with timid but determined courage, the last sentence threw Charlton for a moment. He could break her arms as easily as thin twigs. She ought to be terrified, begging him not to touch her. Dimly he began to realise that whatever it was he was chasing seemed to matter much more than he had guessed. The threat — perhaps even the actuality — of violence might not be the way.

"Suppose I told the police about it?"

"You've got nothing to tell them." The reply was too quick, too defensive.

"Oh, I don't know. There was more to it than just her becoming a Catholic. I gathered that much. The police might want more details. You'd have to talk to them."

He was fishing and he knew it, but there had to be something there. Then Ruth asked a question which shook him.

"Did you kill Martha?"

"Did I what?" He sounded disbelieving. "Of course I bloody didn't! Why should I?"

"Because . . ." Ruth hesitated. Did it make sense that Charlton would have killed her? It certainly would not have helped him discover anything. But perhaps he had threatened her as well. Perhaps he had gone into the studio that afternoon and challenged her the same way he was doing it now. Perhaps Martha had defied him — Martha had been afraid of nobody — and he had lost his temper. He was frighteningly strong.

"You'd deny it anyway," she argued defiantly.

Charlton leaned forward. "Just get this into your stupid head. I didn't kill Martha. I heard the crash from the top of the garden and saw you run from the cottage and followed you."

"But if it wasn't you and it wasn't me, then who was it?"

"It wasn't anybody! It was an accident."

He was saying the same thing. An accident. An accident that someone had almost wanted to happen. Ruth needed time to think.

"I don't want to talk about it now. Come back this evening. I'll be here."

Charlton's eyes narrowed. Instinctively he knew she would not go to the police; she had been too obviously scared when he said that he might do so. For a moment he considered bullying her again, but decided it would achieve nothing, at least not for the moment. She might talk to the others, but he had once seen off half a dozen drunken skinheads causing trouble at the fair. A bunch of old age pensioners would present no problems.

"But you'll tell me," he prompted. "This evening."

"Perhaps. I need time to think."

"You do that. I don't know everything, but I know enough. The police would be very interested if I told them I'd heard you telling Dorothy that Martha had been murdered. Because you haven't said that to them have you?"

From the moment Ruth had seen him when Dorothy opened the kitchen door, she knew he had been listening. He was cunning enough to have waited with that raised fist, a prepared image of surprised innocence. He must have heard what she said about Martha's death, but obviously he was already sniffing round before that, a rat chasing the scent of some hidden morsel. She was safe as long as he did not go to the police, and that could not have been his intention or he would have done it by now. She did not want to hear what he was plotting; probably he had not yet decided because he was still ignorant of what he was on to.

"Come back this evening," she repeated. "About nine o'clock."

He slid off the chair and she glimpsed the arrogant bully inside the stunted frame as he swaggered to the door. He had tasted power over another human being for the first time and it seduced him like a drug.

"Nine o'clock," he said without looking back. "I'll be here."

Solid, clumsy footsteps faded away as Ruth became conscious of the radio again. ". . . thank you, Martin. And now Beryl Jordan is here with her weekly round-up of the best buys at your local greengrocers. I understand that salad vegetables are well worth looking at."

"Indeed they are, Julia. There's lots about and they're coming down in price. Yesterday I picked up some absolutely marvellous . . ."

Ruth turned the set off and her finger lingered on the button, half disbelieving that the world could be so unaware that her entire life had collapsed and she was silently screaming with the agony of it.

Dorothy Lowe slammed the front door furiously and walked straight to where the whisky stood on its tray in the living-room. She poured the drink with shaking hands, then swallowed it in one heaving gulp. Fortified by neat alcohol, she picked up the telephone.

"Edith? It's me. Dorothy. I've just been round to see Ruth. She's got it into her head that Martha was murdered."

"Oh, no, not again." Edith Hallam-West sounded dismayed.

"Again?" Dorothy demanded. "What do you mean, again?"

"She's already talked to Patrick about it. Hasn't he told you?"

"No, not a word. When was this?"

"I'm not sure. The other day sometime. He only mentioned it to me because I happened to run into him."

"For God's sake!" Dorothy shouted frustratedly. "What's he keeping it to himself for?"

"He thought she was being hysterical. Told her to forget it."

"Well she hasn't forgotten it."

For a few moments both women were silent, then Edith spoke again.

"But why can't she just accept it was an accident? That's what happened."

"She doesn't believe that. We should have realised she wouldn't."

"But it *was* an accident! The police have told her."

"That makes no difference. She thinks it was too convenient."

"We've got to talk to her," Edith said urgently. "Make her see sense. I'll go round."

"No," Dorothy contradicted sharply. "That will only make her start imagining there's more to it. We'll all talk to her together tonight. At the beach."

"At the beach?" Edith repeated in disbelief. "Is that really the best place?"

"Yes," Dorothy told her firmly. "Tell Edward and Patrick so they're prepared and I'll talk to Belvedere. If we all stand firm and convince her it was an accident, she'll believe us eventually. You know what she's like."

"I know what she was like when Martha was alive. But I'm not sure about her now."

Dorothy hesitated. "All right, she's different at the moment. But that's only because of the way she's thinking. It's understandable. We should have expected she'd react like this. We'll talk her out of it."

"Will we?" Edith asked uncertainly.

"We've got to."

Chapter Thirteen

Tobias stretched contentedly in the sun on the front doorstep, slitted yellow eyes murderously watching an unaware black-backed gull perched on the wall ten feet away. Sharp claws flexed instinctively as he idly contemplated the prospect, but he was warm, comfortable, fed and not in the killing vein. His ears pricked at approaching footsteps and the bird squawked and flapped off. Tobias looked with patronising indifference as the gate opened and Maltravers stepped on to the path.

"O cat." Maltravers solemnly made a slight bow. "You'll have to believe I'd raise my hat if I was wearing one."

Tobias blinked slowly then rolled on his back, condescendingly offering his belly fur to be stroked. Maltravers dutifully obliged.

"Who's that?" Lacey called from inside.

"Only me," Maltravers replied as he straightened up. "I'm paying due respects to your familiar to stop him turning unpleasant."

"Pardon?" Lacey appeared in the doorway. "Oh, that's where he's got to. I thought he was asleep on my bed. Come in. Coffee?"

"Thanks." Maltravers followed Lacey through to the kitchen where he picked up a percolator and a jar.

"Instant or proper? Both come with fresh cream."

"Instant will be fine."

Lacey switched on the electric kettle, spooned granules into two cups then bent down to take a carton of cream from the fridge.

"What are you hiding from me?" he asked quietly.

"Am I hiding something from you?"

"Of course you are." Lacey closed the fridge door. "You've got barriers across your mind like a steel safety curtain."

"Better ask Tobias."

"Oh, I often do. But his communications are not always clear." Lacey regarded him carefully. "You're worried that you may have found the answer and you don't like it, do you?"

"Frankly, it sickens me," Maltravers's acknowledgement was mordant with distaste. "That's why I don't want to say anything at the moment, because the more I think about it, the less I like it. It's a possible connection between Agnes Thorpe's disappearance and what happened to Martha Shaw which makes a perverted sort of sense. No, not sense. Madness."

"An evil madness?"

Maltravers sighed. "That's as good a word as any. But I could be wrong, and for the time being I'd rather leave your mind open to other possibilities. You might come up with a less offensive explanation, which would make me a damn sight happier. In the meantime, I want to check something out. If what I'm thinking won't go away, I'll let you know."

Already half boiled, the kettle gushed steam and turned itself off. Lacey made the coffee and offered Maltravers a bowl of multicoloured sugar crystals. For a few moments, they sipped their drinks in silence.

"Evil seems less potent in daylight doesn't it?" Lacey said finally. "Less easy to believe in. But it's still there."

"I'm afraid it may be," Maltravers agreed. "Come to sunny Porthennis. Bring the children. Sun, sea, fresh air and murder."

"Can you prove that now? Murder?"

"I don't know." Maltravers shook his head and turned away. "Stop mining my brain, Mortimer. I've said I'll tell you when I'm ready."

"All right. Pax. I'll be patient. But what have you come to see me for if not to talk?"

"What was the name of that church you went to in Wenlock the other day and how do I find it?"

"Wenlock?" Lacey repeated. "I wondered when we'd come

back to that. It's Saint Thomas the Martyr's, modern building on your right as you drive in on the road from St Austell. You can't miss it."

"You said you talked to the priest. What's he like?"

"Father . . ." Lacey hesitated as he chased a name. "Father Cassell. We only chatted for a few minutes, but he seemed all right. Youngish, but I've got to the stage where even the police superintendents are starting to look young, never mind the constables. When are you going?"

"Tomorrow. I'll telephone first to make sure he's not on holiday."

"Why not today?" Lacey asked.

"Because there's something I want to do tonight." Maltravers finished his coffee. "I'll see you when I get back from Wenlock."

"I'll be here." Lacey looked at Maltravers very seriously. "I must warn you of something, Gus. I can't say what you're thinking, but right from the start I've been convinced you would be the one who solved this. I'll see if I come up with something else, but however much you dislike whatever it is, I'm afraid it may be true."

"If it is, it's a very . . . nasty truth."

"Well you didn't have to get mixed up in this," Lacey said evenly. "You could have told me at the very beginning that I was off my head or just said it was none of your business. Then perhaps it would have all remained a secret. But it's too late for that now, isn't it?"

Ruth Harvey stood in Martha's studio, weighing the hammer in her hand, smacking the steel head experimentally against her small palm. If she waited behind the back door for him to walk in . . . ? But suppose she didn't kill him immediately? How many more blows would it take? Two? Three? Ten? Bile swirled into her throat and she went faint at the thought of Charlton's defenceless head, blood spurting from crashing wounds. And could she even bring herself to strike the first critical blow with sufficient strength, summoning up enough rage to deny inbred instincts of a lifetime of gentleness? No, of course not. And even if she could, it wouldn't solve anything. She would then have to kill herself and the police would never stop asking questions. And they might discover the truth.

Sadly, she put the hammer down and went back across the garden to the cottage. The idea of killing Charlton had been born out of desperation and because she could see no other way out. But there had to be one. Paying him money was out of the question. There was nearly five thousand pounds of her own in the building society, but Martha had left her nothing but the cottage and only that in trust. She could sell some of Martha's smaller works — her solicitor had discreetly suggested they would fetch good prices — but it was agony to contemplate trading pieces of remembered love in exchange for money. So how was he to be stopped? Because when she had stood in front of Agnes Thorpe's statue again, she had felt Martha telling her that he had to be.

But beyond all this lay the shrieking question of who had killed Martha. Had it really been Nick? Suddenly he appeared as likely as anyone. Ruth Harvey had built her entire life around one other human being and death had left her exposed, frightened and angry. The moment she had seen Martha's broken body, the conviction it had not been an accident had sprung fully formed into her mind and had never left her. Exposing who had done it was more important than any of Charlton's brutal threats. Concentrate everything on that, she told herself, then decide what you must do.

"Belvedere! Are you in? It's me. Dorothy."

"Leave me alone." The crumbling voice from the direction of the studio sounded irritated. "I'm working."

"That'll be the day," Dorothy muttered as she walked through and opened the studio door, kicking a pile of paint-stained rags aside as she stepped inside. Scott was standing in front of his easel, the canvas it held completely untouched. He scowled at her.

"What do you want? Sod off."

"Busy?" Dorothy nodded at the canvas. "Inspiration isn't exactly flowing is it?"

Scott suddenly looked very tired, ancient brown gargoyle

face losing its bitterness at her arrival and withering like a slowly collapsing balloon.

"Go away." It was the nearest Dorothy had ever heard to him pleading. "I can do it if I try hard enough. I just can't remember what the house looked like."

"What house?"

"Where we lived. In Tarascon-sur-Ariège. The bedroom had a white iron balcony, didn't it? We used to stand on it and watch the sun set over the mountains. Do you remember?"

Dorothy stared at him in disbelief. "Tarascon? That was . . . oh, God, don't let's think about how long ago. You can't bring that back."

"But I can paint it."

"Why?" Unexpectedly caught by his mood, she felt closer to him than she had for years. "What's happened?"

"I don't know. I showed someone the old pictures. That must have started it." Scott looked back at the canvas in despair. "I thought I could do it again. I wanted to."

"You left that painter behind a long time ago," Dorothy said softly. "I used to love him." She turned away, unable to meet the terrible sadness in his eyes.

"What's the matter with us?" she said impatiently. "Two boring old fossils getting sentimental. It's ridiculous."

"You're right." Scott hurled his palette down with a clatter, as though abruptly consumed with exasperation at attempting something impossible but irrationally desired. "I'm getting senile. I need a drink."

Dorothy followed him through to the sitting-room, remaining silent as he poured his rum.

"What do you want anyway?" he demanded. The cloak of the irascible, eccentric artist had slipped back into place. "Not like you to make social calls. Not here at any rate."

"It's Ruth," she replied. "She's convinced someone killed Martha."

"Bloody good job if they did." The glass was raised in a token toast. "Good luck to them."

"For God's sake, be serious! We've got to stop her or she'll be blurting it out to the police."

"Let her," Scott replied indifferently. "They're satisfied it was an accident. They'll put it down to hysterics."

"And if they don't?"

Scott was pouring another drink. "No concern of mine. I didn't kill her."

"You'd lie through your rotten teeth if you did." Dorothy spoke with increasing urgency. "Just think will you? Think of what she could say."

"Ruth won't say anything," Scott began to walk towards the door. "If she does, she'll be up to her neck in it as well. Nothing's going to bring Martha back, which is the only thing she wants. Just give her time and she'll get over it."

Dorothy remained in the room as he left. He was quite right. She hadn't thought of it that way, but Ruth daren't go to the police. She was annoyed with herself for not realising that, and Edith had not grasped it either. For the first time in years, she felt affection for the man she had once loved. She walked through to the kitchen where he was helplessly tackling what appeared to be about a month's washing up.

"Let me do that."

He looked surprised, but said nothing as she pushed him to one side.

"Just pile them up," he told her. "They'll dry themselves."

He sat and watched her for a few minutes. "Long time since you've done this sort of thing for me."

"Don't get used to it, but I'm quite grateful to you at the moment. You've actually come up with some common sense for once. About Ruth."

"It's obvious," he grunted. "She was bound to start thinking that way about Martha dying, but she can't really believe it. And even if she does, what's she going to do about it?"

Dorothy felt a twinge in her fingers as she scrubbed something hard, brown and undefinable stuck to a plate. Bloody arthritis. "Probably nothing, but we can't just leave it alone and hope it'll go away. We'll have to present a united front."

"We're good at that. We always . . ."

Dorothy turned round as the uncompleted sentence hung in

the air. Scott was frowning at her dumpy figure bent over the sink, his eyes reflecting a pursuit of memory.

"What is it?" she asked.

"Nothing." He stood up and crossed to the kitchen window. "Just something that occurred to me. Nothing important."

Dorothy recognised a tone she had heard countless times; barriers had come down and nobody would be able to breach them. There were secret parts of Belvedere Scott, jealously guarded and untouchable. Once it had concerned her, but it didn't matter any more.

She finished the dishes and even made an effort to tidy the rest of the wreck of the kitchen before leaving. Alone again, Scott went back to his studio and contemplated the empty canvas before unlocking it from the easel. It had been a mad impulse, a self-delusion that he could miraculously pick up the past and he was over it now. But what he could not escape was the awareness that had come unbidden while he was talking to Dorothy, the cold realisation that Ruth might not be hysterical.

Maltravers saw Nick Charlton for the first time that afternoon. He was sitting on the harbour wall, passing the time until he went to Cat's Head cove, when he heard metal crunch and glass splinter behind him. A BMW travelling too fast through Porthennis — more than ten miles an hour — had met another car on a blind bend, their bumpers locking together. There was the usual exchange of hostilities while traffic built up in both directions before the drivers agreed to move and exchange the necessary formalities. As one cautiously reversed there was a wrench of tearing metal and the BMW driver shouted that he was doing more damage. Further consultation — by now watched by a small crowd — followed and efforts were made to untangle the vehicles, but one bumper was obviously jammed solid beneath the other. As a cacophony of impatient horns echoed in the narrow streets, Maltravers's casual observations heightened as a very small figure appeared out of the group of onlookers. He spoke to both drivers then one went back to his car as the dwarf squeezed himself in the narrow gap between the vehicles and grasped the front bumper of the BMW. As his barrel body tensed, the effort was almost tangible as the vehicle inched upwards. Charlton only held it up for a few seconds as the other car backed away and was clearly relieved to let it drop, but it had been a staggering display of strength.

As the temporary blockage was cleared and traffic began to move again, Maltravers watched Charlton carefully, accepting the thanks of both drivers before walking away down an alleyway. Nastiness added to muscle power like that was a disturbing combination. He would not have needed to push that rock on top of Martha Shaw; he could have done it by just blowing.

Patrick Dawson's face was as hard and impassive as the coal he had long ago hacked out of the rocks in dark, cramped tunnels below Lancashire. His body had been permanently hardened by the experience, but he had got out before the choking black dust had been able to lay the foundations of death in his lungs. Now he was weathered like oak, his only concession to the decline of age a pair of National Health spectacles unchanged for more than twenty years, a strip of grubby sticking plaster holding one arm together. He listened to Edith Hallam-West with the indifference of a man living on a mountain top being told that floods threatened the valley. His mind was more occupied with painful twinges of gout in his left foot.

"I've been over all this with Edward," he said as she finished. "Ruth came to see me first. Is she now saying who she thinks did it?"

"No. I don't know which of us she suspects. Perhaps all of us."

"Let her get on with it then."

"Is that all you can say?"

"That's all there is to say. If Ruth's got it into her head that Martha was murdered, I'm not wasting my breath trying to tell her otherwise."

"But she might say it to other people," Edith argued.

"Deal with that when it happens."

"That could be too late. We've got to do something now."

"Like what?"

The soft, suggestive question hovered in the air, almost as tangible as the haze of slowly swirling blue-grey fumes from his chain-smoked cigarettes. Edith was repelled by the icy, enquiring indifference in his eyes; he looked mockingly amused at her reaction.

"Not that," she whispered.

"Have you got any other suggestions?"

"There has to be one."

"Let me know if you come up with it. You know your way out."

As Edith left in despair, Dawson returned to his work. He had long ago decided that there were only two sorts of things people worried about; those outside their control and those within. If it was outside your control, there was nothing you could do and worrying was pointless; if it was within your control, you did whatever was necessary, however difficult, distasteful or even dangerous, until you reached the point where it went out of your control. Then you were back to square one. He could do nothing about Ruth's suspicions over Martha's death, so he simply dismissed them from his mind; if the situation arose where he would be able to act, he would do so. In the meantime he was not going to worry. Life was too short.

Chapter Fourteen

Placid high-tide evening sea licked and rippled over Cat's Head cove as Maltravers stood on the wide ledge of flat stone at the foot of the coombe leading down from the coastal path, shallow waves softly slapping below his feet. It was possible to go right or left, but either route meant climbing over ranges of smooth, jumbled boulders and did not reach any further down the beach. Younger people might try it, but the survivors of the Porthennis School were not likely to venture further than where he was standing. Ferns nearly as high as his head partly overhung the rock and he carefully pushed them aside before taking a long stride into green denseness; fans of fronds rustled and closed behind him, leaving no sign they had been disturbed. He sat down and was visible only to hawking seagulls lazily looping in the sky above him. It was just after six o'clock, which meant he had about an hour to wait; placing a notebook in readiness on the ground beside him, he took a paperback copy of *A Fatal Inversion* from his pocket and began to read.

Dorothy and Ruth were the last to arrive by the gate at the top of Fern Hill, the others waiting impatiently near their cars as they walked up from Martha's — now Ruth's — cottage. Scott heaved himself from his seat on a stile as they joined the group.

"Let's get it over with," he growled. Nobody else spoke.

Led by Edward Cunningham, the crocodile of three old men and three old women, friendships and passions rusted into indifferent familiarity, went through the gate. Their moods varied. Cunningham and Dawson were asking themselves why they still bothered; the event had become a parody of itself, patronised by later generations as quaint and amusingly sentimental. Edith Hallam-West held on to it for reasons of pride, fierce loyalty and memories of past promises; Agnes Thorpe was not the most important death in her mind as she made her way between hedgerows overlooking peaceful sea. Dorothy Lowe and Scott, walking arm in arm where the path was wide enough, discovered that their mutual detestation of each other and dismissive contempt of the occasion was now replaced by fierce recollections. Ruth Harvey, quiet ghost of Martha Shaw by her side, wept inwardly and outwardly.

When they had begun the annual pilgrimage, they had been in their vigour, conquerable worlds of youth still attainable. Now they had passed through maturity into old age and, beyond the indignity of senility, lurked death. It was a pantomime preserved by perversity. Touching the shade of Agnes Thorpe recreated lost years of hope, ambition and resolution; for a few brief moments they could forget all the things that had not happened and feel again the drive of dreams before they had turned to bitter disillusions. For a few days their sadness would be overwhelming, then they would revert to their adopted roles, hiding personal scars behind carnival masks of eccentricity.

Cunningham led them into the coombe and they cautiously descended, Scott's stick gouging holes out of dry earth as he clumsily manoeuvred his overweight body. On the rock at the bottom, Dawson held out his hand to the others to help them over the last few feet and they stood in a line, panting from exertion as water quietly clopped beneath them.

"Five minutes to go."

Maltravers checked his watch; seven o'clock appeared to be the significant time. As he waited, a centipede silently crawled between valleys and peaks of earth before disappearing into the undergrowth again. He doodled on the first page of his notebook, ears alert for someone to speak again. They had passed within only a couple of feet of him, but he had been unable to see them, only the grunting and gasping of their descent indicating their arrival.

"Seven o'clock," Cunningham said.

Maltravers scribbled a shorthand outline. He recognised the

voice and would also know Scott, Edith, Dorothy and Ruth. Dawson was the only one he had not met. There was silence again as the second hand of his watch completed a single revolution; he wondered if any of them had bowed their heads.

"That's it. And I'll tell you here and now, it's the last bloody time I come here." Maltravers noted the northern vowel sounds and wrote Dawson's name alongside the comment.

Edith answered, dismissive and indifferent. "Patrick, you've been saying that for years, but still you always turn up. We all do. And we probably will until we can't."

"And I've been asking myself why ever since we started."

"And how many times have we been over it?" Edith said impatiently. "Perhaps none of us can explain it now. Not even to ourselves. It's just become part of the way we are. Apart from each other, we've only got memories left."

"I've not got anybody left." The nervousness in Ruth's tearful voice was cutting with bitterness. "Martha's not here now."

"I know. I'm sorry, Ruth." Edith sounded uncomfortable. "Let's have a minute's silence for her as well. Come on, it's the least we can do."

"You hypocrite!" Maltravers tensed as Ruth Harvey screamed the accusation. "I want to know who killed her! I want to know which one of *you* killed her. Which of you pushed the statue over?"

Shorthand outlines raced as Maltravers scribbled, then there was another silence, much shorter than the one for Agnes Thorpe, but filled with a sense of tension that he could almost feel.

"What are you talking about, Ruth?" Edith spoke as though explaining something to a frightened child. "It was an accident."

"Do you really expect me to believe that?"

"But it's true," Edith insisted. "Why should any of us want to kill Martha?"

"Dorothy said she did. That night in the Steamer."

"Oh, Ruth! Dorothy didn't mean it. Come here."

"Keep away from me!" There was a scuffle of feet, then

Ruth's voice spoke again from Maltravers's left, on the start of the ascent up the coombe. "Dorothy said it and you were all there. You wanted her dead!"

"No!" It was Dawson again, harsh and admonishing. "Leave it alone, Ruth. That never happened."

"Who are you lying for Patrick?" Ruth demanded. "Yourself? Was it you?"

"I've not been near your cottage for weeks. I know you're upset, Ruth, but it was an accident."

She ignored him. "Where were all of you that afternoon? Edith said she was going into Penzance, but what about the rest of you? Edward? Patrick? Dorothy? Even you, Belvedere."

"Ruth, stop it!" Dorothy spoke for the first time, her voice tight with agitation. "Stop it at once! You're getting hysterical."

"That's what you want to think, isn't it? Poor little Ruth's going mad." She sobbed violently. "But I'm not. If one of you . . . Martha was all I had! She was . . . You'll never understand. Any of you. God, I hate you!"

"Ruth, you're just throwing out accusations." Cunningham sounded quiet and reasonable. "You're jumping to conclusions because you're upset."

"Don't patronise me again, Edward. You've all been doing that for too many years. I was never really one of you. I know that." -

"That's not true," Edith protested. "You've been here almost from the beginning. We're . . . we're your friends."

"No you're not," Ruth contradicted. "Martha was your friend. She was one of you. If it hadn't been for her, you'd have had nothing to do with me. You'd like me dead as well now."

"If you're going to think like that, there's no point in —" Dorothy began.

"How do you expect me to think?" Ruth interrupted.

"There's no point in trying to talk to you. We can tell you that Martha's death was an accident until we're blue in the face, but you're never going to believe us."

"Dorothy's right," Cunningham said. "How can we prove we *didn't* kill her?"

"That's not reasonable," Edith added gently. "Is it Ruth? Now come on, we don't want to talk about it here. Let's all go and —"

"Oh, no." There was another sound of movement. "You've all worked it out haven't you? How you'll persuade me to forget it. Well I won't. Just stay away from me! All of you."

There was the sound of ferns being thrust aside as stumbling footsteps faded up the coombe. Maltravers heard one of the remaining five sigh heavily.

"Well that got us a long way, didn't it?" Dawson sounded resigned. "She won't listen to sweet bloody reason in this state."

"What else could we do?" Edith demanded. "She's got an obsession about it."

"More than that," Cunningham said quietly. "She could be right."

"Of course she's not right," Dorothy snapped.

"Why not? Let's be honest, none of us is shedding any tears over Martha."

"Do you mean you agree with her?"

"I don't think it's impossible. Does anybody else?"

For nearly half a minute Maltravers's pen poised over the paper; now Ruth had left them, nobody instantly dismissed the suggestion as outrageous.

"For what it's worth, I was in the shop all that afternoon and young Susan was with me. Good witness a vicar's daughter," Cunningham said finally. "Anyone else want to produce an alibi?"

"Don't be ridiculous," Edith snapped. "We don't need alibis."

"Yes we do," he contradicted. "Because if we can all prove to Ruth that none of us could have done it, she'll have to accept it was an accident. What about you Patrick?"

"What time did it happen? About half past four wasn't it? I was out in the van and nowhere near Fern Hill. It's true, but I can't prove that to Ruth or anybody else."

"Belvedere?" Cunningham asked.

"I was asleep." It was the first time Scott had spoken. "I always am in the afternoon. You all know that."

"Yes, but there's nothing to say you didn't get up is there?" Cunningham remarked. "And you, Dorothy?"

"I was at home. Watching television."

"Right next door to Martha's." Cunningham sounded sourly resigned. "You say you went to Penzance, Edith, and the speed you drive means you could have come back at any time. Ruth could suspect any of us."

"For God's sake, Edward —" Edith began.

"For God's sake, nothing!" Cunningham's shout echoed across the cove. "It could have been you or Patrick or Dorothy or Belvedere."

"And you're in the clear," she said bitterly. "With witnesses."

"Only by chance and what use is it? If one of us did it and it comes out, all of us get dragged down as well."

"I'll tell you this," Dawson put in quietly. "If it was me, I'd tell you."

"That's clever, Patrick," Cunningham said, cynically appreciative. "But it could be a double bluff and I'm too old to fall for that. The fact is Ruth thinks Martha was murdered and four of us can't prove we didn't do it."

"So what do we do?" Dawson asked.

"There's damn all we can do. Except try to shut Ruth up."

This time the silence was longer than before.

"I don't want to talk about that," Edith said finally. "I don't even want to think about it."

"We may have to," Cunningham told her. "Anyway, we'll cross that bridge if we come to it. In the meantime, the only thing we can do is carry on as normal. With a bit of luck, everyone will think that Ruth is losing her marbles and won't take any notice. Come on. I need a drink."

Maltravers heard them start their ascent back up the coombe; Scott wheezing with the effort. As the sounds moved away, he flicked back through his notebook, adding occasional parallel lines in the margin to highlight certain remarks. Ruth's accusations had sparked an instant sense of apprehension among the members of the School. Nothing they had said to her or among themselves after she had gone had done anything to undermine his theory. Their acceptance that one of them could have killed Martha Shaw — and the implication that they had some reason for having done so — only confirmed it more.

Once he was satisfied that even the slowest of the Porthennis School would have reached the coastal path, Maltravers stepped out of the ferns and sat on the rock where they had stood. There were still the question of Charlton of course, dancing dwarfish attendance on the School and seen near Martha's cottage in the night. Classified by Helen as nasty, assessed by Lacey as capable of malevolence, that disturbing presence lurked in shadows. He could not share the others' motive for wanting Martha dead . . . but was it possible one of them had used him to kill her? The thought came spontaneously and was instantly persuasive. If paid enough money, was Charlton capable of being a hired killer? Maltravers did not find the idea inconceivable. He wanted to meet him, and Cunningham's final remark about needing a drink suggested at least some of them were by now on their way to the Steamer. Even if Charlton was not there, contact with the others while their emotions were exposed could be revealing.

Putting his notebook away, he climbed up to the path and walked back to Helen's cottage where she and Lacey were waiting for him.

"Well? What happened?" Helen demanded the instant he walked in through the door.

"Patience." Although Maltravers was not looking at Lacey, he could feel his eyes concentrating on him. "Perhaps another half step forward and the theory still hasn't collapsed. They've gone to the Steamer and I want to join them there and need you two with me."

Helen stepped forward and put her hands on his shoulders. "What is it Gus? Mortimer says you won't tell him. Why not?"

"I've been through that with him," Maltravers replied. "Just hang on until I'm certain."

"I warned you Helen," Lacey said quietly. "Gus's mind has gone into hiding. He'll come back to us eventually."

Helen half crossly ruffled Maltravers's hair. "There was a time when you and I didn't have secrets."

"True," Maltravers acknowledged. "But we always trusted each other. And we still do. Come on, I don't want to miss them at the pub."

They were approaching the Steamer when Maltravers paused. "Assuming they're here, there's something I want to poke around a bit. It may be important. Let me do the talking, and don't look too shocked at anything I might say."

The Steamer was quieter than usual and almost the first customers they saw were Scott, Dawson, Cunningham and Dorothy, with Charlton sitting next to them. There was no sign of Edith or Ruth. Helen and Lacey joined them as Maltravers ordered drinks and took them to the table. For a while they chatted about nothing in particular — nobody mentioned having just returned from Cat's Head cove — then, as the conversation flagged, Maltravers casually turned to Lacey.

"I see that car workers' strike's ended with the unions getting a bloody nose. Another victory for Maggie, thank God."

Helen had to control herself. Maltravers was a political atheist, sharing Claud Cockburn's belief that whenever you were talking to a politician, your constant thought should be why the bastard was lying to you. An amused contempt for any party meant he had not voted for years. Overt appreciation of Margaret Thatcher — or someone diametrically opposed to her Conservative philosophy — was like hearing him express support for child molesting.

"Think that's a good thing do you?" Cunningham's voice had an instant edge of hostility, which Maltravers either did not hear or ignored.

"Don't you?" he asked calmly. "The unions have all been taken over by the Militant Tendency. Everyone knows that. They were ruining this country until the Tories sorted them out."

"So you'd rather we were ruined by the rich then? That's what Hitler wanted."

"Oh, come on." Maltravers gestured disparagingly. "It's not the same thing. You can't say that beating the Nazis meant we had to be taken over by someone else instead."

"Remember the war, do you?" Cunningham had turned in his seat to face Maltravers aggressively. "Were you even born?"

"No, but my father was killed in it."

Helen looked down at the table to stop anyone seeing her face. She had been very fond of Maltravers's father, a civilised and amusing English teacher; he had died of cancer in 1980.

"And you like to think he died so that Socialism could be destroyed?" Cunningham demanded. "We were fighting for something better than the poor being kept in their place."

"The poor are always with us," Maltravers replied indifferently. "Joining up in 1939 and fighting right through to 1945 couldn't alter the facts of life."

"It should have done," Cunningham replied. "And some of us started fighting long before 1939."

"International Brigade?" Maltravers sounded vaguely interested but not impressed.

"That's it," Cunningham confirmed. "So was Patrick here. And a lot of other good men. We could see what was happening long before the rest."

"But you lost that one," Maltravers remarked. "And Spain didn't do badly under Franco. The Communists never got control and now they have a monarchy again. Hardly worth bothering was it?"

Helen jumped as Cunningham slapped his hand hard against his thigh with a hollow metallic clang.

"Hear that?" After the emotional gathering on the beach, Maltravers had swiftly pushed him into anger. "Hear it? What used to be there I lost at Guadalajara. But I killed at least three Falangists first. And I didn't do it for another generation of bloody capitalists!"

"It was all a very long time ago and I didn't come in here to have a row." Helen had sensed the gathering forces behind Cunningham from the others. "Can we drop this please, Gus?"

"Yes of course," he said, glancing at Cunningham. "We're never going to agree anyway. Sorry. Let me buy you a drink."

"I've had enough." Cunningham stood up, false leg manoeuvred with years of practice. "Goodnight."

"Anyone else then?" Maltravers broke the awkward silence that followed his departure. "Another rum, Belvedere? Dorothy, what will you have? Refill for you, Nick? Same again, Patrick?"

Charlton shook his head, but the others seemed to accept that he was trying to make up for the anger caused by what he had said and told him what they wanted. Helen went with him to the bar.

"What the hell was that about?" she whispered angrily as he waited to be served. "It was sick. You sounded like a Fascist."

"It was all an act," he murmured. "You know that well enough."

"They didn't think so."

"That was the idea."

"And where's it got you?"

The barmaid came up and Maltravers ordered before replying. "Things keep repeating themselves."

"But how does baiting Edward about the war help sort out who killed Martha?" Helen demanded.

"He brought in the war, I just followed him," Maltravers corrected. He picked up the first glasses the barmaid brought him. "Here you are. Take these and I'll bring the rest. Don't worry. I'm not going to start any more rows."

When he returned to the table they had relaxed again, but Charlton appeared on edge, mean eyes restless, pudgy fingers constantly fiddling with his glass. As the rest of them talked, he suddenly finished it in a series of noisy gulps and dropped from his seat to the floor.

"Thanks a lot," he said. "But I've got to go. See you."

Maltravers and Lacey watched him push his way to the door, clumsy and childlike between other customers, then glanced at each other. Lacey's mouth twisted with distaste and his nostrils flared, as though catching an unpleasant smell. Scott was grumbling about an argument over prices with a printer who was producing a series of postcards from his paintings and Helen was making sympathetic noises. Dawson had remained silent since Cunningham left and Dorothy Lowe appeared to have withdrawn into herself. The conversation stumbled uncomfortably along for about twenty minutes before Helen said supper would be ready. They left the three remaining artists apparently settled until closing time.

"You were playing with fire in there," Lacey remarked as they walked away. "If you'd told us what you were going to do, we'd have warned you about Edward's temper."

"Did you pick up any thoughts from him?" Maltravers asked.

"Oh, yes," Lacey confirmed, "but they were very confused and there was nothing I didn't know already. Edward's always resented the fact that losing his leg in Spain meant he couldn't fight the Germans." He glanced at Maltravers. "And you don't know how close you came to having Dorothy going for your throat. Metaphorically speaking now, but once upon a time she'd have done it literally."

"Was she in Spain as well?"

"No, but she and Belvedere met in the 1930s when he was living in a village in the Pyrenees," Lacey explained. "During the Occupation they fought with the Resistance. Sabotage, reconnaisance for the Allies, helping escaped prisoners of war, you know the sort of thing. Some of their friends were caught and tortured before being executed."

Maltravers was silent for a moment, then said reflectively, "And fifty years don't wipe out memories like that."

"No they don't," Lacey agreed quietly. "And you don't forget being raped by the Nazis either. There were seven of them."

"Oh, Christ!" Maltravers stopped and closed his eyes as if in pain. "Judge not that ye be not judged."

"What do you mean?" asked Helen.

"That when you know the reasons for what people do, you can at least understand, even if you can't forgive them."

A spasm of silent shock flickered across Lacey's face. He had been watching Maltravers very closely and mental guards had fleetingly dropped. Lacey said nothing, but suddenly understood a great deal.

"What about Nick?" he asked. "Where does he fit into it all?"

"I'm not sure," Maltravers replied. "But when I'm ready, I'll need to ask some direct questions to sort that one out. I wonder where he went in such a hurry?"

"Oh, I can tell you that," Lacey said. "He was going to see Ruth. I don't know why, but that much was clear enough."

"To see Ruth?" Helen turned to Maltravers urgently. "Gus, if you know so much, you've got to do something. She's on her own."

"It's all right," he assured her. "Whatever he's gone to see her for, it can't be to kill her. If she died now, so soon after Martha's death, the police would start digging up the drains and nobody wants that."

"Do you mean it was him?" Helen demanded. "He killed Martha?"

"He could have done." Maltravers kicked a stone lying on the path. "All I know is that somebody did."

"Stop it!" Helen took hold of his hand fiercely. "No more secrets, Gus. Not now, I can't stand it. You've got to tell us."

"Because your theory keeps standing up, doesn't it?" Lacey added quietly. "It all goes back to Agnes Thorpe."

Maltravers shook his head at him helplessly. "I had a feeling I let it slip just then. I could almost feel you grab on to it. Yes it does, and what I overheard on the beach virtually clinches things. If I can find out what I want to know in Wenlock tomorrow, I think I'll have just about all the pieces."

He turned to Helen. "All right I'll tell you, because I can't see any other answers now."

In bed that night, Helen lay awake for a long time, trying in vain to comprehend the minds of people she thought she had known.

Chapter Fifteen

Vivid and angular, abstract patterns of stained glass gleamed
in windows framed by biscuit-brown brick walls as Maltravers waited for the priest in St Thomas's. The pews were
pale polished oak set on a floor of large square slabs of dull
silver and aquamarine stone; a twenty-foot symbolic Christ
crucified in polished steel hung suspended from wires behind
the altar; wherever there were not pastel colours there was
white paint. Unlike Lacey, Maltravers had no feeling of the
presence of Martha Shaw or anyone else; as an almost devout
agnostic carrying a belief that he would die convinced of his
doubts, he was detached from any inherent spirituality of
serious houses on serious ground, dark and cobweb ancient
or bright ultra-modern. While driving the fifty miles to Wenlock, he had repeatedly gone over how he could approach
the problem; the sanctity of what might have been said in
this building would be inviolate, but perhaps he could extract
enough information to make almost the final moves along a
tortuous path.

"Mr Maltravers?" The priest had approached from behind,
rubber shoes soundless in the silence. He was about forty,
faint cadences of Ireland audible in the dark, courteous voice.
He was wearing charcoal-grey trousers and a blue cotton shirt
that had not been ironed properly, topped with a grubby
clerical collar, and his hair needed cutting. "I understand you
wish to talk to me."

"Father Cassell?" Maltravers stood up and held out his
hand. "Yes I do. It's a rather delicate matter."

"If you wish to take confession we can —"

"I'm not of your faith," Maltravers interrupted. For a moment the priest looked at him.

"Then perhaps we should talk in my study."

The study would have presented Hercules with a demanding thirteenth labour for an encore. Two walls were lined with overflowing chipped whitewood bookcases, volumes of theology, lives of saints, biographies of Popes, meditations for the Godly, pamphlets and magazines shelved, piled and crammed together. Between boxes of old clothes, parcels addressed to Third World missions and a wondrous collection of second-hand furniture, a narrow path snaked across the floor to a desk where a wooden crucifix stood precariously on top of a sliding hill of littered papers. Every horizontal surface — window sill, seats of chairs, untrodden floor around and beneath furniture, tops of bookcases — bore its share of bric-à-brac. No woman would have tolerated it, but vows of celibacy meant that Cassell did not have a wife to organise him.

"Excuse the mess." The apology was as automatic as a reflex response during the enactment of a familiar church ritual. Cassell picked a pile of papers from a cane-bottomed straight chair, looked around uncertainly then balanced them on top of eight boxes already leaning like the clock tower at Pisa. Maltravers accepted the vacated seat and the priest stepped across other obstacles to sit at the desk.

"So how can I help you?" he asked.

"First of all, I should explain that I am not from the police or any other authority," Maltravers admitted. Cassell bowed his head in silent acknowledgement. "I'm just a private citizen who has become mixed up in something and I think you may be able to help." He unzipped a document case. "Do you know Porthennis at all?"

"As a visitor, although it's some years since I've been there."

Maltravers produced a copy of the *Independent*. "There's something in this I'd like you to look at. Page fourteen."

He passed the newspaper over and watched closely as Cassell turned the pages. The priest glanced over the whole page, then momentarily stopped as his eyes reached the bottom before looking back at Maltravers enquiringly.

"It's about the lady in the last obituary," Maltravers said. "The one with the picture. Have you seen her recently?"

Cassell looked down at the paper again and hesitated before replying cautiously. "I . . . think I may have. She looks like . . . one of a number of people I may have spoken to recently."

"And presumably it would have been here," Maltravers added. "She lived in Porthennis and you say you haven't been there for some time."

Cassell's lips pursed suspiciously. "Did you trick me into admitting that, Mr Maltravers?"

"Not at all. You volunteered the information. But it means that if you did see her, it must have been here . . . at this church?"

Cassell handed the newspaper back. "I haven't precisely told you I have seen her. And before we go any further, I would like to know why you are asking these questions."

"I don't expect you to tell me things without some explanation," Maltravers replied. "Obviously, the lady is dead. It's being put down to an accident, however I have . . . let's say reason to think she may have been murdered."

"Then you should not be talking to me. You should go to the police."

"Perhaps. But I haven't got enough evidence yet, and I'm also not sure that involving the police would be the best thing to do."

Cassell paused again. "You've told me you're not a Catholic, but I presume you know that a priest respects all confidences. Totally." It was a tacit invitation. Maltravers smiled slightly.

"It's a very strange story. I haven't come to your church by chance but because of a man who knows things he shouldn't."

The priest's face held nothing more than attentive interest as Maltravers explained about Mortimer Lacey's visit to St Thomas's and why he had made it. When he had finished, Cassell looked out of the window as though assessing it all.

"Your friend sounds a very interesting person," he said finally. "And . . . yes, I think I can go as far as saying the lady came here once. But I don't see any way in which I can help you."

"You can by answering one more question," Maltravers told him. "When Martha Shaw came to this church, did you take her confession?"

"If she did — *if* she did — then I could not tell you or anybody else what she might have said. I rather assumed you'd realise that."

"Of course I do, but that's not what I'm asking. All I want to know is if she *made* a confession, not what it was."

"I don't think I could even confirm that. The fact that someone is seen entering the confessional does not automatically mean they wish to make confession. They may be seeking a blessing, or even just want to chat to the priest. These days it's as much to do with counselling as admission of sin and its forgiveness."

Maltravers's chair creaked protestingly as he leaned back. "Could we talk about that? Absolution of sin? Purely hypothetically."

During the next hour Martha Shaw's name was not mentioned as Cassell discussed the beliefs and practices of his church, Maltravers constantly questioning him. At one point the priest smiled.

"For an agnostic, you know a lot about religious faith," he said. "You argue theology very well."

"You don't have to go to church to think about or even believe in God," Maltravers replied. "Tell me more about the Catholic view of repentance."

Neither seriously disturbed the other's beliefs, but at the end both were left with things to think about. Cassell had clearly enjoyed the conversation as much as Maltravers.

"You should meet my bishop," the priest remarked. "He'd have made some points much better than I have, but you'd have still argued with him, wouldn't you?"

"Of course. You should examine your reasons for being an agnostic as much as you should ask yourself why you're a churchgoer. If you can't defend it, you can't claim it as a faith."

"Agnosticism as a faith?" Cassell shook his head. "An interesting thought. I'll be quite honest, Mr Maltravers. There are many practising Catholics who could not justify their belief as well as you defend what they would see as a total lack of it."

"Thank you. And now that we understand each other a little better, can I ask that question again? Did you take Martha Shaw's confession?"

"I knew you'd come back to that." The priest sighed. "I could suspect you of being very clever, but I rather think you're sincere. All right. Yes, she did . . . but you'll get no more out of me."

"I don't need any more, Father. I'll tell you what she confessed."

Cassell's face remained totally impassive as he listened, then he looked at his watch and stood up.

"I can make no further comment, Mr Maltravers. I wish you well in your investigations, but I cannot help you any more than I have. Perhaps I've even gone too far as it is. Now if you'll excuse me, I'm due at one of our schools shortly."

"Thank you for your time." Maltravers smiled. "You know, if you hadn't been a priest, you'd have made a great poker player."

"I'll accept that as a compliment," Cassell said, and accompanied him outside to his car.

"There is one other thing," Maltravers added as he was leaving. "If I get to the bottom of all this, I'll come back and tell you the full story, unless you'd rather I didn't."

The priest shook his head firmly. "I'd rather you didn't. I think it might . . . trouble me. I think it might trouble you, Mr Maltravers."

"You could be right."

Maltravers drove out of Wenlock and on to the open wildness of Bodmin Moor; there was no immediate urgency to return to Porthennis and he wanted time to think. He parked on a high bare hill and walked to where a group of huge rugged rocks capped its peak and climbed the jagged face of the biggest. Sitting on the top, he stared across interlocking folds of smooth green moorland, washed with sunshine blotted by wind-driven shadows of cloud. He now knew why Martha Shaw had made the journey to St Thomas's, which Lacey had traced with his strange abilities. Cassell had in no way acknowledged that what Maltravers claimed she had confessed was correct, but it had to be. And it was understandable she would have wanted to tell a stranger anonymously, not the Penzance parish priest who knew her. From his conversation with Cassell, it appeared he would have been able to grant her absolution of the sin within the laws of the church, but would also have advised her to talk to the police. Was that what she had decided to do? And had she told someone of her intention? And had that person murdered her?

Maltravers stubbed out his cigarette, grinding black ash on the rock's surface. He now had enough to go in direct pursuit, trying to disentangle the identity of a murderer from a swarm of suspects. Deliberately he stopped himself trying to guess which one it was, because there were now no innocents. For a long time he had clung to the possibility that the statue that killed Martha Shaw could have fallen accidentally and Lacey suffered from hyper-imagination. That way normality lay and Maltravers had wanted to believe it; but now he could not and was left with something malignant. And a murderer who could eventually kill again? It was a dreadful possibility, but, presented with nothing more than Lacey's psychic powers and Cassell's unbreakable vow of silence, what action could the police take? At this stage it was impossible to name the killer and Maltravers had to continue probing until he knew. Then he might have to go to the police, but was increasingly convinced that he would prefer not to.

Mortimer Lacey came out of the front door of his cottage as Maltravers walked down the path outside Lifeboat Row and met him at Helen's gate.

"Well?" he asked.

"The priest was discreet, but told me enough," Maltravers replied. "You were right. Martha did go there. She went to make confession."

"I presume he didn't tell you what it was."

"No, and he gave nothing away when I told him what I'm positive she must have said. But I've got to be right." Maltravers looked at Lacey unhappily. "It doesn't happen in places like this."

"It's troubling you, isn't it?"

"Cassell said it would and I agreed with him. I just didn't realise how much."

Lacey touched his arm reassuringly. "I'm afraid that any powers I have are woefully limited and I don't see any way I can help at the moment."

Maltravers sighed. "You've got me into this, Mortimer. If it hadn't been for you, I'd have accepted like everybody else that Martha died accidentally. Where are you now I need you?"

"You don't need me," Lacey contradicted. "At least not at the moment."

"You're a very present help in time of trouble," Maltravers told him sourly. "Incidentally, I've learned something else as well. On the way back I called in at the offices of the *Cornishman* in Penzance and had a chat with the editor."

"Do you know him?"

"No, but I still do occasional freelance work and journalists will always talk to each other. I wanted to know when Martha Shaw's inquest was being held. It's in a couple of days, but he also told me the police are satisfied it was an accident. Nobody gains from her death, nobody had any motive."

"Not that they can see," Lacey observed.

"No," Maltravers agreed. "You don't expect people to be murdered because they have found God. Anyway, the final step is talking to Ruth. She's the only one who knows who can also be ruled out as a suspect."

"But which of the others was it?" asked Lacey.

"I've got one name in the frame, but it's no more than an educated guess," Maltravers told him. "It could have been almost any of them."

"Plus Nick Charlton," Lacey added. "He's in there somewhere."

"I'm not absolutely sure of that any more."

"Well I am, and he's the one you should be very careful with. There's your evil."

"There's part of the evil," Maltravers corrected.

Maltravers walked up Fern Hill, unlatched the cottage gate and walked up the path. He rapped on the brass knocker cast like a leaping dolphin and waited for a few moments, looking across the garden at the studio, wooden walls blotched with huge sun-baked blisters of paint, cracked open and gaping like leprous white blossoms. He heard the door open behind him and turned round to face Ruth Harvey; she looked like the walking dead.

"Hello," he said gently. "We've met before. By Agnes Thorpe's statue at the Botallack the other night. Augustus Maltravers."

"Pardon?" She seemed confused. "At the . . . ? Oh, yes, I remember. There was a young lady with you."

"That's right. Tess Davy. We were talking about Martha. That's why I'm here."

The grief on her face turned to fear and her voice pleaded in terror as she backed away from him.

"No. Please go away. I don't want to . . . Not you as well. Who are you?"

"A friend of Helen Finch's," he replied, projecting reassurance and comfort into his reply. "You know Helen. Don't worry, I'm not going to harm you. In fact I think I may be able to help."

Red-rimmed eyes blinked in dazed bewilderment as he stepped through the doorway and took her arm. She made the slightest movement of pulling away, then allowed him to lead her into the front room. He made her sit by the window then pulled up another chair and sat very close to her, holding her hand.

"It doesn't matter how I've found out what I know," he said. "I just need you to tell me certain things. I can't promise to solve everything, but I rather think you're more a victim of all this than anyone. Let me tell you what I know then I have just a few questions."

At first she would not speak, slender, exhausted face unreadable as he gently explained what he had first guessed at, then investigated. Only when she began to grasp that he knew a great deal, did she begin to respond, tears slipping down her cheeks. Then came the anguished replies and small corrections of fact made in tiny whispers. As it all came out, he could feel the relief pouring from the little woman that at last she could talk about it.

"There's just one final question," he said at the end. "I've been told that a man called Jonathan Bright was a member of the Porthennis School, but I don't know anything about him. What do you remember?"

"Jonathan?" Ruth frowned as though puzzled. "I don't know very much. He was Polish and changed his name when he was sent here as a refugee in 1939. He went back after the war, but his family had disappeared so he returned to Britain. He came here because Frank Morgan invited him. I couldn't understand why, because he was a very poor artist."

"How did Frank Morgan know him?"

"They both belonged to some debating society in London. Frank used to go up every month for their meetings."

"Do you know what sort of debating society?" Maltravers asked. Ruth shook her head.

"I never took much interest. It was called . . . oh, it's so long ago . . . the Fourth International or something like that. But why do you want to know about Jonathan? He died years ago."

"It was just an odd loose end in my mind." Maltravers reached across from his seat and took her hand. "Thank you. I'm sorry I had to come here, but I knew you were the only one who would tell me."

"What are you going to do?" She did not look at him as she put the inevitable question.

"Everything I can to help *you*," he assured her. "It depends on other people of course, but I think I can sort it all out . . . well as much as it can be sorted out now."

"And what about Nick Charlton?"

Maltravers had been so involved in unravelling the last strands of the mystery, that he had failed to realise that Charlton's name had never come up.

"What about him?" he asked.

"You see, you don't know everything," she said sadly. "He's been threatening me."

Maltravers sat upright and looked at her closely. "What have you told him?"

173

"Nothing . . . well no details," she replied. "I've managed to put him off so far. But he knows things and has threatened to come back and make me . . ."

Soft tears were suddenly overtaken by a shudder of wracking emotion; she clasped her hands to her face and her little body shook as she wailed under the weight of insufferable terror. Maltravers waited for her to recover; dealing with Charlton had suddenly become a matter of urgency, but he had to reassure her he would do it before leaving.

"I didn't know what Nick Charlton was doing," he said as she dropped her hands back into her lap and looked at him beseechingly. "But you have my word that I'll sort him out. Just tell me what he knows."

"He's only guessing really," she replied. "But he came here and . . ."

When Maltravers left the cottage he was seething with anger; his immediate desire was to find Charlton and hit him with any available blunt instrument. But that would solve nothing. As he walked back down Fern Hill, he began to calm down as he worked out what he had to do. Ruth had given him the address and he made his way past holidaymakers strolling through the streets of Porthennis, children's laughter in another world, towards the street behind the harbour. He reached the front door and stood on the step for a moment controlling himself.

"Don't lose your temper, find it," he muttered, then deliberately held down the bell push, thumb tip white with pressure.

"All right, all right!" Charlton's voice called from inside the cottage in irritation. "I'm bloody coming!"

He half opened the door and looked at Maltravers aggressively. "What the hell's the matter? What do you want?"

"To talk to you," Maltravers pushed him aside as he kicked the door open and stepped inside. Caught off balance, Charlton staggered backwards and stumbled, swearing as his head caught the skirting board. Maltravers slammed the door shut and looked down at him. There was apprehension in the dwarf's mean, cunning eyes.

"Get up," Maltravers ordered and walked across the room, grubby wallpaper, paintwork seamed with dust, steaks of dried dirt on the windows and a smell of mustiness like rotting fungus. Charlton cautiously rose to his feet, watching him warily.

"I know you," he said. "You were in the Steamer the other night. With Helen Finch and that puff Lacey. Who the hell do you think you are, barging in here and —"

Maltravers sensed the gathering of animosity to mask fear and instantly stamped on it.

"That doesn't matter," he snapped. "I know who you are and I know what you are, and either I'm going to sort you out or the police will."

He picked up a wooden dining chair and hurled it across the room. It hit the wall and fell at Charlton's feet.

"Now sit down on there you little shit!"

When Charlton did not immediately obey, Maltravers grabbed a heavy slate clock off the mantelpiece and menacingly took half a step forward.

"On the chair, or I'll bloody brain you!"

Charlton's token resistance collapsed as he scrabbled for the chair, eyes never leaving Maltravers, and sat in it like a mechanical doll whose spring has suddenly broken.

"That's better." Maltravers weighed the clock in his hand for a moment. "I've been talking to Ruth Harvey and she's told me things about you that I don't like. I presume you know that blackmail is a very serious crime."

"I've not been blackmailing anyone," Charlton muttered defiantly.

He yelped and ducked in terror as the clock crashed against the wall inches from his right ear, gouging a deep, jagged hole in wallpaper and plaster. There was a tinkle of shattering glass as the brass front swung open on its hinge. Before he could move, Maltravers had leapt forward and retrieved the clock and was back where he had been standing.

"Don't kid yourself I missed," he warned. "I could have hit either one of your balls at this range. Any more stupid lies like that and this thing takes your goddamned head off."

175

For a moment Charlton stared at him then managed to give the impression that he had shrunk even smaller than nature had made him.

"What do you want?" The question held the right level of fear.

"You're going to tell me everything you know. And don't leave anything out because, believe me, I'll know if you do." Maltravers was satisfied he had scared Charlton enough to bluff him.

"I don't know that much . . . No!" Charlton stiffened and held up both hands defensively as Maltravers raised the clock again threateningly. "OK, I picked up a few things here and there and realised there was something they wanted to keep quiet."

"What was it?"

"I couldn't find out. Then Martha died and I know Ruth thinks she was murdered. It had to be tied up with the others somehow."

"So instead of going straight to the police, you decided to threaten Ruth and force it out of her," Maltravers observed caustically. "Bloody charming. Good at pushing old ladies around aren't you? Don't like it when it happens to you though, do you? What else did you find out?"

"That's all. Honest. I know nothing more than what I've told Ruth and if you've talked to her . . . She said she'd tell me more later. When she'd had time to think."

"Ruth's told me about that," Maltravers agreed. "I had the feeling you hadn't got all that much, otherwise you'd have been even nastier than you have been. Christ, you're disgusting."

Charlton turned away as Maltravers looked at him in distaste. "Anyway, you've got it round your neck. I know the full story and there's nothing for any of them to worry about. But they're old and they get confused. Ruth's distressed about Martha and went haywire when you started poking your filthy nose in."

"But there's something," Charlton insisted. "There has to be."

"Of course there's something," Maltravers acknowledged. "But nothing really important. Certainly not Martha being murdered. That's crap. All the police are going to be interested in is the fact that you've been blackmailing Ruth Harvey. I'll enjoy being a witness at your trial. It should take you out of circulation for a while. Your best bet will be pleading guilty and hope the judge takes it into consideration. But there's some big lads in the Scrubs or wherever they send you. Very fond of old ladies and don't like little turds who molest them."

"I never touched her!" Charlton protested.

"We've only got your word for that," Maltravers replied coldly. "But I might add a few bits and pieces to my evidence. I'm good at telling stories."

He turned away indifferently, putting the clock back into place. Now everything depended on Charlton being so confused and afraid that he would not suspect Maltravers was lying. And when it came to Charlton being jailed for blackmail and his treatment in prison, he wasn't. In the pecking order of convicts, sex offenders lay at the bottom of the pile, despised by other prisoners and persecuted whenever possible.

"I've not actually done anything," Charlton said hesitantly. "I've never got any money out of her. And I've never hurt her. She'll tell you that. I'll . . . I'll back off."

Maltravers did not look at him. "What do you mean?"

"I mean that . . . for fuck's sake give me a break! I'll make it up to her, I'll look after her. There'll be no more —"

Maltravers whirled round. "If you even so much as walk up Fern Hill again, I'll make sure you're inside before your feet touch the ground! You stay well away from Ruth Harvey. You've done enough bloody damage."

"What the hell do you want me to do then?" Charlton protested. "Or are you just going to turn me in? Whatever it is she's frightened about, it's going to come out if you do."

Maltravers paused then nodded. "All right, you've got a point. It doesn't matter that much, but Ruth's been through enough lately. Let me think a moment."

Charlton watched anxiously as Maltravers went silent. Cornered by threats with enough truth in them to carry weight, he would now accept almost any alternative to escape a blackmail charge. Maltravers was calculating the terms he could impose; they had to be severe enough to suggest he was totally serious, but not impossible.

"All right," he said finally. "I don't approve of letting criminals off, but I expect it's the lesser of two evils. I won't tell the police, and you get the hell out of Porthennis."

"What do you mean? Move?"

"I'm not talking about a world cruise. Clean this place up a bit and you'll get a decent price for it. Then find yourself somewhere . . . let's say at least three hundred miles away. Property's cheaper in the North. And don't come back here for your holidays."

"I don't want to leave here."

"Try that line on the judge when he sends you down for five years or whatever it is," Maltravers smiled cynically. "Appeal to his better nature."

Charlton glared at him for a moment. "Can I trust you to keep quiet?"

"As long as you do as you're told," Maltravers assured him. "I'll give you six months top weight to sort it out. I'll check with the people I know here and if you aren't celebrating the New Year far enough away for my peace of mind, I'll drop you right in it. Got it?"

"Bastard." The insult was muttered so softly that Maltravers ignored it. "All right, but if you screw me up I'll shoot my mouth off about everything I've picked up. I mean that."

It was a pitiful last flash of aggression, but Maltravers had won every round and was prepared to grant Charlton the empty satisfaction of childish defiance at the end.

"Don't worry," he said. "I've got better things to do than bother with scum like you. Keep your nose clean and move and I won't give you any grief. Remember that I know people here who'll tell me if you step out of line."

He crossed the room to leave, Charlton watching him cautiously.

"I saw you pick that car up by the harbour yesterday afternoon," he added as he opened the door. "Very impressive, but as you see I don't scare easily. Don't get any stupid ideas about waiting for me down dark alleys, because I've seen off better than you."

He slammed the door again as he left. Once he was out of

sight round a corner, he closed his eyes and gave a long shuddering sigh of relief. His best chance in a physical encounter with Charlton would be the fact that he could run faster. The dwarf had been a one-man audience to a spurious hard man performance Tess would have applauded; thankfully, he appeared to have fallen for it.

Now all he had to do was find a way of protecting Ruth Harvey from other dangers before trying to identify a murderer.

Chapter Sixteen

"The first thing we have to do is convince Ruth that Martha died accidentally. Right?"

Maltravers looked round the room enquiringly. Since Tess had returned from the Botallack an hour earlier, the four of them had discussed how they should handle the situation. Nobody had suggested going to the police; the tacit agreement that they would not was absolute and unquestioned.

"But how do we do it?" Tess asked.

"Mortimer could probably persuade her," Maltravers said, turning to him. "But you already knew I was going to say that, didn't you?"

"Yes," Lacey agreed absently. His ink-coloured eyes looked very far away. "I can tell Ruth things about herself that will surprise her very much indeed. I think she'll believe me."

"Perhaps I can help there as well," added Helen. "I know her better than you."

"We'll go and see her together."

"Good." Maltravers stretched out his arm and picked up Helen's gin decanter. "Then she can start letting it go and perhaps find some peace of mind. After that we clamp the lid on this can of worms very tightly."

Tonic water fizzed as he dropped ice into his drink and swirled it reflectively in the glass.

"Tomorrow's Saturday," he said. "You two go and see Ruth first thing, but then we've got to get the rest of them together and show them we know the truth. That's going to scare them rigid. We then offer to keep quiet about it on the strict understanding that they leave Ruth alone. But how do we get them together?"

"Tomorrow evening's no problem," Helen told him. "Edith is holding a private viewing and sale at her studio. They'll all be there. They always support each other on occasions like that."

"What about Ruth?"

"She usually goes, but I can't see her turning up this time. Perhaps we can keep her away in any case."

"Leave that with me," Lacey put in.

"All right," said Maltravers. "What time does the viewing end?"

"Nine o'clock. Then they'll probably go to the Steamer."

"Well they'll certainly need a drink by the time I've finished with them. I'll turn up for the last half hour or so which will look innocent enough at first."

"I'm coming with you," Helen told him. "In various ways they're friends of mine and I'm not having them think I couldn't face this."

"Of course. And I want you there as well, Mortimer. You'll know the moment anyone starts lying."

"But which one?" Lacey wondered.

"You've no ideas?"

"No. It could be any of them."

"And meanwhile I'll be exchanging Noël Coward *bons mots* at the Botallack," Tess said. "I don't think my mind will be on my job."

"I'll tell you everything when I pick you up," Maltravers promised. Including, he thought to himself, what I can't tell you tonight.

Waiting for Lacey and Helen to return from seeing Ruth the following morning, Tess and Maltravers went down on to Porthennis beach again. The tide was out and they walked nearly a mile along the coast, scrambling over rocks until they reached a promontory from which they could see across to Cat's Head cove in the distance. High on the headland beyond it, the top of the Botallack's stage was just visible in a shimmer of heat haze. Tess sat down and Maltravers knelt on a patch of sand in front of her, focusing his camera.

"Move to your left a bit," he said. "I want Cat's Head in as well."

"Hardly your average holiday snap," Tess remarked as she shuffled to one side. "It's macabre."

"Ain't that the truth?" There was a click as he pressed the trigger then he lowered the camera, winding on the film as he continued looking at the scene he had just recorded. "I'm just praying that Mortimer can pull it off with Ruth. She's got to believe the accident story."

"But who *did* murder Martha?" Tess asked. "We know so much, but can we ever really find that out?"

Maltravers closed the camera case and sat next to her. "That's why I want Mortimer there this evening. He'll know."

"But you might not be able to prove it."

"Does it matter?" He picked up a flat stone and sent it skimming across the flat, placid sea. It bounced across the water leaving a wake of shining circling ripples before dropping out of sight with a tiny splash. "What's important now is not that Martha died, but that Ruth lives."

When they returned to the cottage, Helen and Lacey had returned and were waiting for them.

"He's done it," Helen assured Maltravers. "It was unbelievable what he told her. There were things that even Martha didn't know."

"I thought it best to go over the top," Lacey added. "By the time I'd finished, she'd have believed me if I'd said Martha committed suicide."

"How was she when you left?" Maltravers asked.

"Tearful," Helen replied. "But I think it was relief as much as anything. She never wanted to believe Martha had been murdered, but it wouldn't go away. We told her you'd spoken to Nick Charlton and that she needn't worry about that any more either. I'll keep an eye on her."

"Let's hope for the best then." Maltravers felt unexpectedly tired as he flopped down on the chaise-longue. "Now we wait until tonight."

Lazy with sunshine, the day dragged by. Tess started learning her lines for a new play at Watford Palace, Maltravers forced himself, without much success, to concentrate on finishing another chapter of his second novel, Helen pottered in her studio. Lacey spent most of the time sitting with Tobias on his lap, gazing out of the window. Occasionally the cat growled restlessly in sleep. The population of Porthennis changed again as more holidaymakers arrived to replace those going home. Gleeful children swam and paddled in the sea, mothers explored unfamiliar kitchens of rented cottages, fathers carried in luggage, a honeymoon couple had their first married row, then made it up in bed.

In Penzance, Nick Charlton sat in the still centre of the spinning roundabout, imagining what he would like to do to Maltravers but afraid of trying it and bitterly accepting he had no choice but to leave Cornwall. Ruth Harvey clutched the comfort of what Lacey had told her with the total acceptance of a child being assured there really were fairies. She picked up a framed photograph of Martha Shaw and pressed her lips against the glass, grief and rage softened by what she did not know were kindly lies.

In the evening, Maltravers drove Tess to the Botallack, then returned to collect Helen and Lacey. They hardly spoke as they fortified themselves with a drink then walked through the village to Edith Hallam-West's studio. The private showing had attracted a reasonable number of tourists and red stickers were on several paintings, indicating they had been sold. The rest of the Porthennis School chatted to the customers, all politeness, subtly persuading them to buy works by their friend. Edith seemed to be everywhere, now discussing birds with some woman, now smiling at Helen, now writing out a receipt. Lacey's eyes casually wandered over all of them, and Maltravers noticed them harden occasionally as though he had become aware of hidden things. By ten to nine, only one couple remained, obviously hoping for a final free glass of wine. When it was not forthcoming, they left and Edith shut the door.

"More than eight hundred pounds," she announced. "That's the best yet. Thank you."

She turned to Helen, Maltravers and Lacey. "Officially we're closed, but you can help us finish the wine."

"Count me out." Cunningham started towards the door. "I want a pint. I'll see you in the Steamer."

Maltravers stepped in front of him. "Hang on a few minutes. I want to talk to you. All of you."

"You've done enough talking," Cunningham told him sharply. "I'm not going to listen to another bloody lecture on trade unions."

"Then how about a lecture on murder?"

Maltravers spoke loudly enough for them all to hear and the sense of relaxation that had followed the end of the viewing snapped into tension. Lacey had positioned himself by one wall from where he could see everybody and Helen leaned with her back against the door on to the street. For a moment, Cunningham looked as though he would push his way past Maltravers, but Edith took his arm and stopped him.

"What the hell are you talking about?" he demanded.

"Don't pretend not to know. It's too late for that now."

Satisfied that Cunningham was not going to try and force his way out, Maltravers looked round at the others. Scott was still in the chair he had occupied since they arrived, the ageing, crumbling idol awaiting gestures of respectful attendance. Dorothy Lowe was holding a handful of Edith's catalogues which she had been collecting from around the room. Dawson stood by the bay window, rolling yet another cigarette. As Maltravers caught the eyes of each of them, they looked away uncertainly.

"First of all, I've got some good news for you," he said. "Ruth now accepts that Martha Shaw's death was an accident. You've got Mortimer to thank for that. Never mind how he did it, it's been done, so you can all stop worrying about it."

"Martha's death was an accident."

Maltravers glanced at Edith. "Was it? Ruth didn't think so, did she?"

"She's hysterical," Edith said dismissively. "I don't know what she's been saying to you, but I'd advise you to ignore it."

"No," Maltravers corrected. "You *want* me to ignore it."

Cunningham's simmering resentment suddenly exploded. "For Christ's sake, I'm not listening to this! If you want to poke your nose into Martha's death, there's nothing I can do about it, but leave me out."

"It's not Martha's death I want to talk about." Maltravers stared at Cunningham until the artist turned away, then he looked slowly at the rest of them. "I want to know which one of you actually murdered Agnes Thorpe."

In the stunned silence, none of them noticed Lacey's burning eyes flash across all their faces; then he gave the faintest nod.

"For no particular reason, my first guess was Belvedere," Maltravers continued. "But then I remembered that you'd been a Commando, Patrick, and a quick death with your bare hands would have been best. I don't imagine she felt anything."

Dawson showed no reaction as he dropped his lighter back into his pocket. A stream of smoke rose from the cigarette in the centre of thin lips. He did not look at Maltravers.

"It doesn't matter, of course, because all of you had agreed it had to be done," Maltravers added. "You were each as guilty as the killer. Agnes had the money to finance your dream of Porthennis as a cultural centre for the people. True Leninist Communism in Cornwall. But suddenly she was going to marry Robert Jenkins, a typical capitalist, the sort of man who'd be destroyed in the world revolution you were certain was coming. That was all that mattered. After she disappeared, the suicide note turned up, allegedly in her handwriting. But Edith is a calligrapher as well as a painter and there would have been no particular reasons for the police to call in experts."

"Do we have to listen to this nonsense?" Edith demanded.

"Nobody goes through that door until I've finished," Maltravers replied levelly. "I'll begin with you Edith, because you were the one who started me thinking when Tess and I met you at Seal Bay."

She looked defensive. "I didn't tell you anything."

Maltravers picked up a straight wooden chair and turned it round, sitting with his arms leaning on the back.

"You told me a great deal," he contradicted. "You met your husband at Cambridge in the 1930s and went to the Black Sea for your honeymoon. Later I learned you both paid several visits to Russia before the war. And some of the KGB's best spies were recruited at Cambridge in that period. And the Germans — the Fascists — killed your husband and children in the blitz."

He looked at her. "Was your husband recruited by the Russians, Edith? Were you?" Bitterness flared in her face, but she did not reply.

"Well, you'd never tell would you?" Maltravers shrugged. "You also told me some things about Patrick which I enlarged later. Born in the slums of Salford, father died in the pits, a member of the International Brigade fighting Franco in Spain with Edward. Hardly the life of a true blue Tory."

He shifted in the chair to face Scott and Dorothy Lowe. "Meanwhile, you were both in the French Resistance and Dorothy was raped by the Nazis. Even the ones who died were the same. I've not seen the originals of Frank Morgan's Belsen paintings, but his soul is in those canvases. And so's all his hatred. It's very understandable that the experience made him a Communist. And he was the one who brought Jonathan Bright here after they met as members of some society called the Fourth International. It doesn't take much to work out that that was probably dedicated to producing the successor to the Third International which the Russians dissolved in 1943.

"The weakest links were Martha and Ruth, because neither had suffered the way the rest of you did. But Martha was under Morgan's spell and Ruth was in love with Martha. They'd have gone along with you, in the same way Agnes did when she wanted your help in making her own dream of a theatre come true. But then she betrayed your dream. She wanted to take her money out of the communal pot and add it to the wealth Robert Jenkins had accumulated on the backs of his workers."

His gaze moved over them all. "My God, you were true believers. And you've kept your faith. Marx would have been proud of you."

It was Edith who finally broke the uneasy atmosphere that settled on the room as Maltravers finished.

"You're too young to know anything," she told him contemptuously. "Do you have any idea how many innocent men and women died at the hands of Fascism? Have you the least conception of how evil capitalism is at its heart? They ate *rats* in Stalingrad to defeat Hitler! Go and stand at the war memorial in Moscow and see if you can face the ghosts of twenty million war dead, more than all the other countries of the world! Some of those people were my friends — and friends of my husband — and they are the ones I have kept faith with. Who are you to mock that?"

She spread her arms to include the others. "We have all kept faith as Fascism has been reborn again and again. It's a battle that may never be won, but some of us will never stop fighting it, however old and weary and . . ." She shook her head helplessly. "No, it's pointless trying to explain. People like you never understand. I can see it in your face."

She turned from Maltravers as though he were an alien being and he knew there was nothing he could say. They had a dogma as fervent and incorruptible as Rome's and arguments about democracy, individual freedom and human rights would simply be explained away by the party line or dismissed as temptations of capitalist devils. Tanks in Hungary and Czechoslovakia were totally justified, Poland an aberration and *glasnost* and *perestroika* weasel words of betrayal. They had grown old, but had not changed, their belief more durable than the Berlin Wall.

"But Martha lost your faith and found a new one, didn't she?" he continued as though Edith had not spoken. "One that involved confession of sin, not perhaps your sin, but it had become hers. That's what you quarrelled about in the Steamer. Martha's Catholicism and your Communism were the immovable force and the irresistible object. She was saying her conscience gave her no choice. She had to expunge her guilt for her part in Agnes Thorpe's murder and was trying to persuade you to do the same.

"So eventually she went to confess it to a priest. I've been to see him. He was not in a position to tell me everything, but I know he would have granted her absolution, and also urged her to tell the police. She made it clear that was what she intended to do. The only thing stopping her doing it immediately was that the statue for Westminster Cathedral was not finished. Then she died. Is it any wonder that Ruth thought she'd been murdered?"

"But had she?" It was the first time Dawson had spoken.

"Frankly, I'm not sure," Maltravers admitted. "But the other night when Belvedere was drunk in the Steamer he was rambling on about someone called Nancy and how something wasn't his fault. Nobody seemed to know who Nancy was, but Belvedere invariably uses the diminutive. Edward becomes Ted, Dorothy is Dottie, Edith is Edie, Martha was Mattie. So I looked Nancy up in a dictionary, and she turned out to be Agnes."

He looked at Dorothy. "You left the pub just before closing time that night, and you could have heard Belvedere. Dangerous talk that. And on the way home, Belvedere fell down the steps." Dorothy looked away as Maltravers turned to Scott. "You showed me where you fell. A level stretch about six feet long. If God really looks after drunks and little children, you should just have collapsed in a heap. Did you fall Belvedere? Or were you pushed?"

"I was pissed." Knotted knuckles tightened on his stick handle. "But somebody pushed me. Couldn't see who it was in the dark."

His head slowly revolved towards Dorothy. "It was someone small and wearing a dress."

Dorothy shrugged. "You were drunk."

Maltravers looked from one to the other. Friendship, art, love, war, unswerving commitment to the cause, murder; Belvedere and Dorothy Lowe had shared a great deal. Suddenly he lost his temper. Like many easy-going men, Augustus Maltravers erupted violently if pushed beyond a certain point.

"Christ, you're pitiful!" he shouted. "You patronise Ruth and she's the best human being among you! You've lived here for years believing that come the glorious revolution you will bring art to the masses whether they want it or not. You killed Agnes Thorpe because she didn't agree with you and forty years later one of you could have gone into that studio and murdered Martha. Did you?"

Nobody replied, but Edith Hallam-West looked at him sharply as though something had occurred to her. "Mr Maltravers, I'd like a private word with you, please."

"What about?" he snapped.

"Just do me the courtesy of listening. It will only take a moment." She went and stood by the flight of open wooden stairs leading to the flat above her studio. "It is important."

Maltravers hesitated a moment, then followed her. On one wall of her sitting-room was a framed poster of Lenin, flying like a god above cheering marching workers; others collected such things as pop art, but for Edith Hallam-West it was an icon of untainted faith.

"I'm going to ask you to keep anything I say confidential," she said as she closed the door. "In any event, I would deny it."

"I don't think you'll need to."

"We'll see." She paused as if sorting out something in her mind. "Frank Morgan used to call me the intelligence of the Porthennis School. My husband taught me how to spot weaknesses in an argument. I think you're bluffing."

"Go on." He did not contradict her.

"Obviously you've spoken to Ruth, who must have told you a great deal," she said. "But you still have to ask who killed Agnes. Ruth doesn't know that does she?"

"No," he acknowledged. "Not even Martha would tell her which of you it actually was."

"So what are you left with? You don't know if Martha was murdered — perhaps she wasn't — and you don't know who killed Agnes. All you have is some clever theories — and I'll admit you've been very clever — and Ruth's hysterics. Not exactly proof, is it? You're no threat to us."

"Oh, I'm afraid I am," he replied. "Because Martha did tell Ruth one very important thing."

A few minutes later they went down to the studio again. During their absence, its occupants appeared to have remained as still as the wildlife frozen in paint around the walls.

"May I have a cigarette, please?" Edith asked him. "I don't often, but I think I need one at the moment."

"Of course." He offered the packet then held his lighter forward. She held the cigarette with the tips of her fingers, pulling her head back sharply as it ignited.

"Thank you." She smiled thinly and went to stand by Dawson.

"Edith will tell you what we've been talking about." Maltravers lit his own cigarette. "She accepts that I could go to the police with what I know and all of you could end up in jail."

"And is that what you're going to do?" There was resignation in Dorothy's question, as though a very long journey was finally over.

"No," Maltravers replied. "What would be the point? In a few years you'll all be dead and in the meantime you'll have to live with the fact that we know your secret. All that concerns us is Ruth. She's not totally innocent, but she's a damn sight less guilty than the rest of you. She knew Agnes had been murdered but had nothing to do with it. After all she's gone through, she deserves to live out her life in whatever peace she can find."

He left a deliberate pause as he looked for an ashtray, crossing to a table by the door when he spotted one.

"So leave her alone. Understand?" He reinforced his order with a flash of anger in his voice. "She now believes Martha was not murdered and won't talk to anyone about Agnes because that would bring out Martha's guilt as well. She has other friends — Helen for a start — and they'll look after her."

"Yes I will." Helen spoke very quietly, but with an undertone of fierceness. "I didn't want to say anything until Gus had finished, but I want to tell all of you now that I cannot understand you. Artists should create, not destroy. For appearances' sake, I'll still chat to you in the Steamer or wherever, but I'll be doing it for Ruth, not any of you."

There was absolute silence as Maltravers opened the door for Helen and then he and Lacey followed her out of the studio and walked away. None of them spoke until they reached the harbour wall and leaned against it, each wrapped in their own thoughts.

"All right, Mortimer," Maltravers said finally. "Who was it?"

"Patrick," he replied. "You were quite right there. And Dorothy killed Martha."

"Shit." Maltravers's voice was dead. "I really would have preferred that one to have been an accident."

"What's our position in law?" Helen asked. "If anything ever comes out aren't we in some sort of trouble for not telling?"

"I don't know and I don't care," said Maltravers. "That won't keep me awake at nights. Ruth Harvey might, though."

"We'll look after her," Lacey assured him. "They've got a few other secrets that they don't want to come out. Believe me."

"I believe you." Maltravers turned round to look at evening light smothering the quiet rooftops of Porthennis climbing from the sea. "It's everything else I don't believe. Now I've got to go and collect Tess and tell her what she doesn't know."

Applause rippled up from below the cliff out of Maltravers's sight as the final performance of *Private Lives* reached its end. A few minutes later the car-park was filled with chattering people, laughingly quoting fragments of lines, reminding each other of moments of amusement. Doors slammed, engines roared into action and for twenty minutes he was surrounded by activity and noise. Then the last cars drove away and silence settled on the Botallack again. He was standing in front of Agnes Thorpe's statue as Tess joined him.

"How did it go?" he asked.

Tess shuddered. "Don't ask. I forgot my lines three bloody times. I've not done that since I left RADA."

"Oh, dear." He smiled sympathetically. "I trust the others closed ranks."

"Wonderfully," she said feelingly. "Neil was magic, but I could see how worried he was. I told them afterwards I wasn't feeling well. All I could think of was what you were all doing. How did it go?"

"They'll do as they're told." He took hold of her hand. "And it could have been worse for you out there tonight. There's something I haven't told you."

She frowned at the seriousness of his voice. "What?"

He looked back at the statue. "Her body is in the plinth."

Tess made a raw sobbing sound and he put his arm around her as she turned away abruptly. For a moment she trembled and did not look back as he led her away.

"How do you know?" Her whispered question was compelled by a perverse desire to pursue an unspeakable truth.

"Martha told Ruth and Ruth told me," he replied. "Edith challenged me this evening by saying that I had no absolute facts to prove anything. But that body means I have. God knows where and how they hid it for however long it was, but when Martha made the statue they hollowed out the plinth and put her inside. Then they probably filled it up with concrete. At least they brought her home to her theatre."

"I've been asked to come back next year," Tess said. "I told them I didn't think I'd be able to. Now I'm certain."

As Maltravers drove away, the last light of day died in the sea and the features of Agnes Thorpe's statue became veiled in darkness and solitude until only a black stone figure gazed towards the empty stage. In the crowded, noisy, laughter-filled bar of the Steamer, Belvedere Scott held rum-drunken court. Asked where the rest of the Porthennis School were, he said they had not felt in the mood that evening. But they would be there again soon.